Bea
Christmas wish

*To: Kaya and Mikaela,
two amazing sisters!!!
With love,
[signature]
2020 Dec.*

For my daughter Bizou and my family

Gwim Philipp

Bear and Nosey's Christmas Wish

A quest filled with adventures

Illustrated by
Jacqueline Molnár

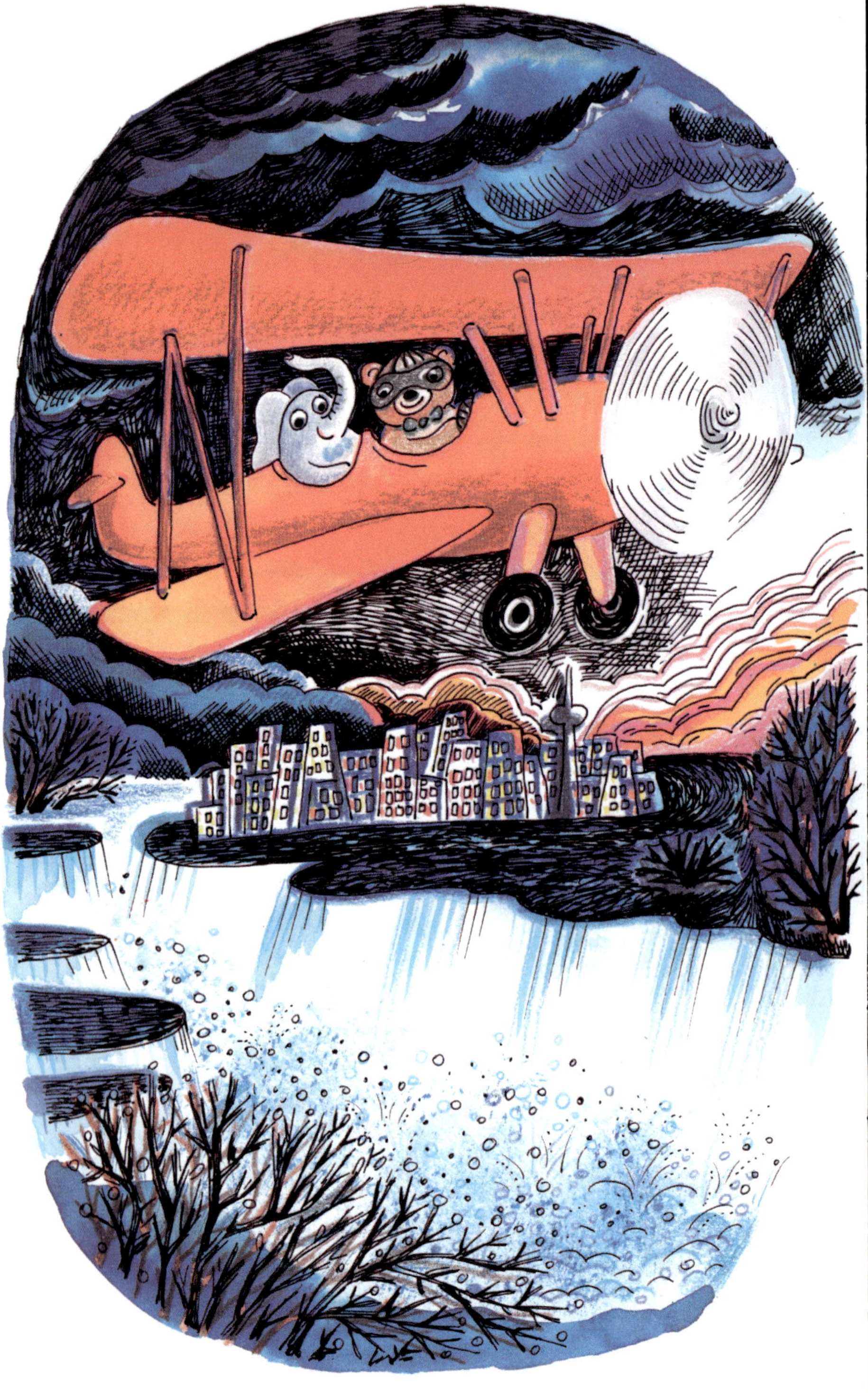

Chapter One

Bear McQueen and Nosey Land in Burlington
...because where else would a grizzly land in Ontario?
Part 1

Bear McQueen's aviator goggles were getting foggy and he had the enormous responsibility of landing the plane. His full name was Knox Ursus Horribilis McQueen, Bear McQueen for short, known for his inventiveness and ability to get out of a jam. His friend Nosey was all cozy in the passenger seat. He was just playing away, drawing snowflakes on the window with his trunk by scraping frost off the windowpane. He was very clever with his trunk, and that's how he got his nickname. His friends simply called him Nosey or Nose. Trunky just sounded weird. His real name was Marcus Aurelius Loxodonta, far too long and pretentius for such a warm, sweet, kind-hearted, little elephant. He had already created three huge beautiful snowflakes, and he was very proud of himself. He flapped his ears and turned to his friend with his characteristic goofy smile, waiting for a compliment. "That looks great, Nosey, he said, and realizing that he had put his goggles on earlier just to entertain his friend, Bear McQueen threw them aside. It was time to land. They had flown all the way across the Atlantic Ocean, where they had escaped from a toy store, and their long trip was almost behind them.

"Nosey, watch this!" he cried out in his shrill voice.

Bear made a big turn with the airplane and they could see the city below magically glimmering in Christmas lights at dusk.

The animals landed at exactly 4:00pm, got out of the plane and rushed through the small airport. All they could think of was getting their paws on some hot chocolate, really fast.

They got their drinks and sat down next to a vending machine, enjoying every delicious slurp. Nosey blew dozens of air bubbles into his hot chocolate with his straw one last time, and then, they got on their way.

They had to find a place to stay before dark

... How exactly the animals ended up at Spencer Smith Park, no one really knows. Some grandmothers claim that they saw a teddy bear and an elephant on a horse and carriage, atop the haystack; others say they hitched a ride on one of the Santa Claus Parade floats. Nosey is absolutely sure they walked all the way, and Bear... well, he comes up with a new story each time.

The animals climbed to the top of the structure in the park and watched the seagulls above Lake Ontario. The air was quite chilly, and, except for a few joggers, they were alone. The sun had already gone down and Bear was making plans.

"First, we must decide on a street."

"How about Grizzly Avenue, Nosey? Or better yet, Horribilis Crescent?" he asked. He thought of himself as a mighty grizzly bear and knew that the Latin name for grizzly bear is Ursus arctos horribilis.

Nosey shook his head. Nosey often nodded or shook his had while he was daydreaming, but this time he looked serious about his opinion.

7

"How about Maple Avenue? Every Canadian city has one."

Nosey nodded this time, and pointed at a street sign in the distance that read "Maple Avenue."

"This will be fun," said Bear, and they slid down the centre bar and arrived in the sandbox with a big thump. They headed towards Maple Avenue hopping happily.

"We're almost there," whispered Bear to his friend.

They saw rows of townhouses with friendly lit windows and silhouettes of people moving around behind the curtains and blinds.

"How are we going to get in, Nosey? And what if we're thrown out?" Bear wondered, but he was optimistic. He continued making plans.

He saw a big cat sitting in front of a closed door, wagging its tail and flexing its claws. It soon produced a shrill "Meow." After three meows the door opened, and it walked in comfortably, with a satisfied grin on its face. The door closed behind it.

"That's it, Nosey! I'll meow, and we'll sneak in." Bear said with excitement, and with this, the two animals started practicing meowing, under a maple tree.

"You'll be the door and I'll be the cat," said Bear.

Bear sat down facing his friend and, just as he had seen the cat do it, he went through the three steps of meowing.

"First, wag the tail," he said, focusing hard.

"Nosey!" he cried out, "They forgot to sew a tail on me." He giggled, but went on to the next step anyway.

"Flex the claws." he whispered.

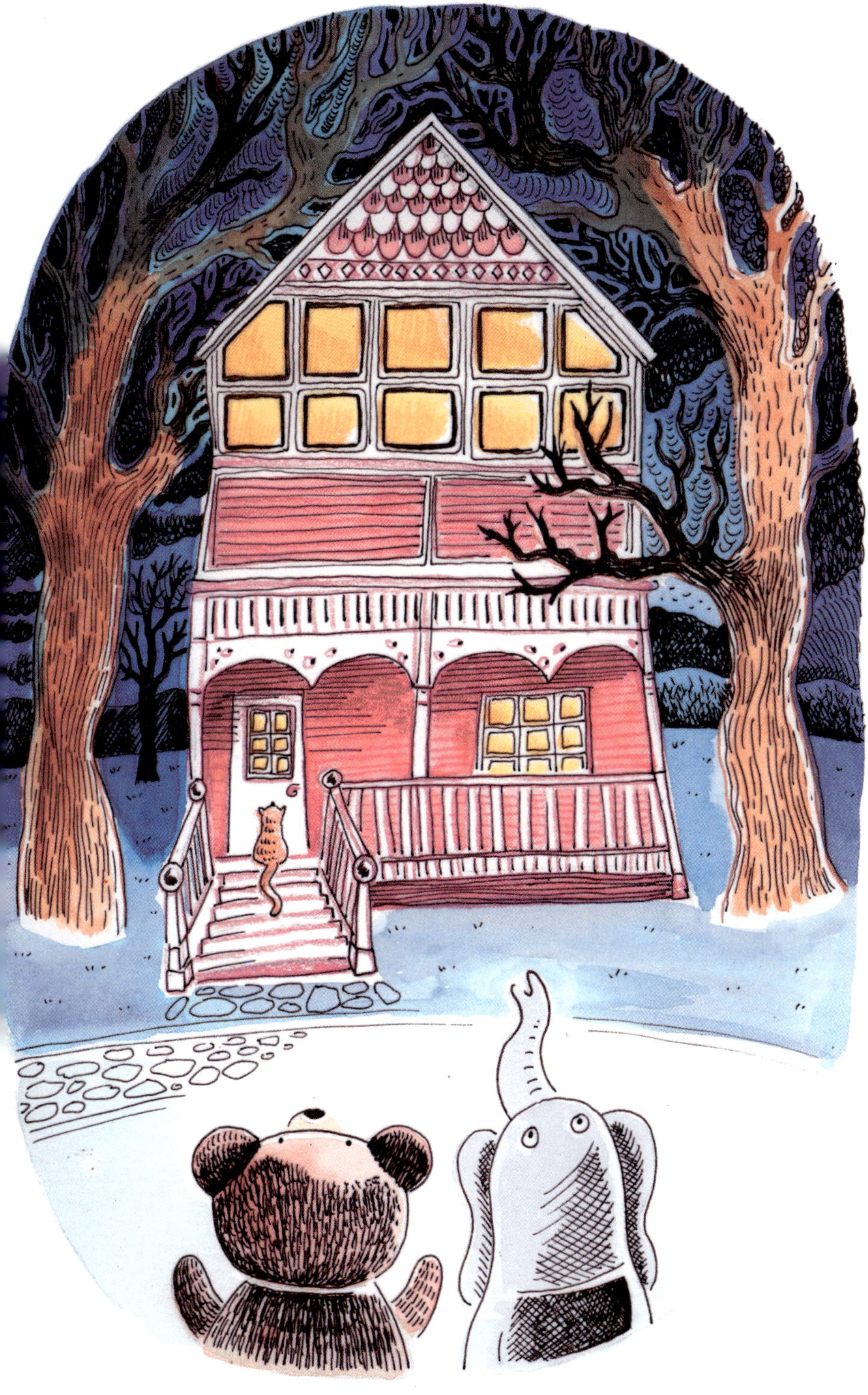

He looked at his paws where his claws should have been sewn in, and laughed.

"Nose, what kind of a bear am I? I don't have any claws to flex, either."

Luckily, he remembered that he could meow as annoyingly as any cat, at least, that's what he'd been told.

"Nothing missing from my famous meow," giggled Bear joyfully, and with Nosey still sitting patiently in front of him, he straightened up and let out a great big "meow".

"This will work. All set," he told Nosey. "You can stop being the door now."

They went to the house where the cat had been meowing. Nosey hid behind a flowerpot and started wagging his tail faster than ever. Bear sat in front of the door. He tried to look as much like a cat as he could, and went through the steps of meowing.

"No tail: no problem," he started.

"No claws: no problem," he went on.

"And drumroll..."

Quickly adjusting his winter tie, he lifted his head slightly towards the stars.

Bear produced a perfect "Meow"...

...and nothing happened.

The animals looked at each other.

"Now what?" Nosey flapped an ear and looked questioningly at his friend.

"If we make grunting noises like elephants, people are not very likely to invite us in. And barking is absolutely out of the question," Bear continued, as he remembered how his barking had once sounded more like a startled mouse.

"Whatever that sounds like..." and his thoughts drifted away to the time when he had been practicing animal sounds in the toy store.

"How about disguising ourselves as burglars?" Bear asked, and looked at Nosey.

But he saw clearly that even a mask wouldn't hide his friend's kind, tame look.

"Maybe in a year or two..." Bear was trying hard to teach his friend to be scary and mischievous, but had not been successful so far.

Now, Nosey had an idea.

"Through the chimney!" he said pointing at the closest one with his trunk.

"That's a neat idea. We'd be just like Santa," Bear squeaked with joy.

But then he thought of all the soot they would be covered in and realized that leaving enormous black paw prints all over the place would hardly be a good idea if they wanted to hide in the house.

They passed two more homes and as they approached a third, Bear exclaimed, "Hey, check this out, Nosey!"

He pointed towards a heap of furniture and cardboard boxes in front of a house. The animals went closer and they spotted a half-closed travelling chest that was overflowing with all kinds of toys and exciting objects. The blue wing of an airplane was jutting out one end, and red and white badminton rackets out the other.

"Looks like some cool people are moving into this house," Bear said confidently, "so we will just move in with them."

Part 2

The animals sat down and entered into a lively debate about how to get into the travelling chest. It obviously held lots of treasures, just the kind a bear and an elephant would wish for.

The chest was much too high, though. It was stacked on top of several boxes, so no matter how high Bear tried to jump, he couldn't even come close to reaching it. Climbing up seemed like a good idea, so they looked for a ladder. They searched all around, but they found nothing they could use. Bear was getting a bit disappointed, but true to his bear nature, he produced a mischievous smile and said, "We must find a way. A bear never gives up." He then continued thinking harder than ever.

"We will get into this chest, no matter what."

He looked around and noticed a tree with its branches hanging above the chest.

"That's it. We'll just have to climb the tree and jump straight into the chest," he said happily, but turning to Nosey, he saw he was worried. He understood right away. Elephants couldn't climb trees like grizzlies could...

"It's OK, Nosey," he said, "I would never leave you behind, you know that. We'll just have to find another way." To prove to his good friend that he really didn't need to worry, he was ready with a new plan in seconds.

"I think I've got it. We need two buckets, a pair of scissors and some strong string. Nosey, you find the buckets, I'll look for the scissors and some string." With this he ran off and soon returned with scissors, pulling a spool of kite string behind him. He also found a few small toys he thought he would surprise his friend with.

Nosey was waiting for him, a little sad because he couldn't find a real toy bucket. All he could find was an old pot with a handle similar to that of a bucket.

"Look here," Bear said, and to cheer him up, he pulled out a bubble-blowing bottle and showed him how to blow bubbles.

"You can play with it, but don't wander off, OK?" he said, and then he disappeared again.

Nosey climbed into the pot with his new toy, and just as he was trying to blow his first soap bubble, he heard a shrill voice from somewhere above him.

"Nosey, here!"

Bear had managed to climb the tree and jump on top of the chest.

"You'll soon be up here, too."

His friend had no idea how he would get up there, but he trusted Bear, so he waited, sitting patiently in the pot, blowing bubbles. As he lifted his head and looked up between two of the nicest bubbles he had created so far, he saw a thin string beside him. He followed the path of the string. It was tied to the handle of the pot he was sitting in. It led all the way up to the tree branch over the chest, looped over the branch and went down again to the opening of the chest where it was tied to a yellow beach bucket. Next to it, Bear was grinning happily, ready to jump into the bucket.

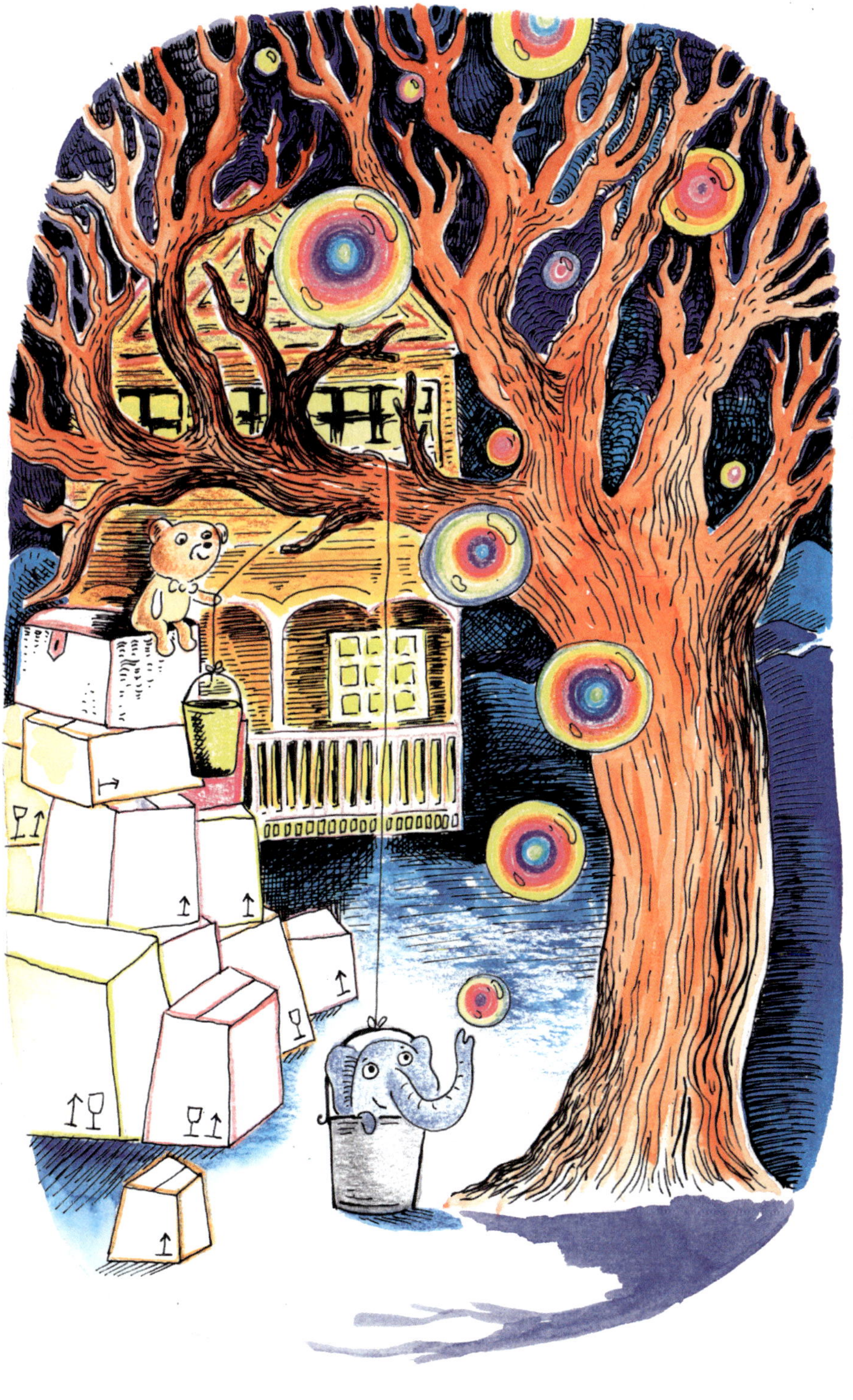

"Watch this, Nosey!" he cried. "We have an elevator!"

And he jumped in, thinking that his weight would pull Nosey up while he himself would travel towards the ground. He couldn't have been more wrong though, and he found himself dangling halfway between the chest and the ground. The yellow bucket hadn't moved down a single bit, so Nosey didn't get pulled up to the chest, either.

"Now what?" asked Bear, trapped in midair, trying to look as positive as he could because he didn't want to worry his friend.

Bear adjusted his tie and cut himself loose with the scissors, landing next to Nosey with a big thump. He was ready to make this elevator work. His friend watched him eagerly. He even forgot to blow bubbles.

An enormous bag of flour, lying nearby, was the key to Bear's new plan. He reconnected the buckets and hauled the bag of flour up to the chest. He then started pouring its contents into the bucket.

"It works!!!" he cried excitedly, as he saw Nosey slowly being lifted off the ground.

Bear jumped down into the pot next to Nosey, and in an instant, they were both moving up towards the chest.

"This is fun!" the friends rejoiced. Bear was very satisfied and Nosey was flapping his ears and waving his trunk from side to side like never before.

The animals jumped into the chest and danced around, celebrating their victory. Then they plopped down on a couple of beach pillows inside the chest and noticed something that lit up in the far corner of the chest.

"Let's check that out, Nose!" said Bear.

But by the time Bear finished his sentence, his friend had fallen asleep and once Nosey was asleep nothing could wake him up. Bear looked at him caringly, but he too was tired, and so he followed his friend's example. Soon both animals were asleep next to each other, dreaming about boats and planes and toys, while enormous and magical snowflakes started falling and the whole city went to sleep.

Chapter Two

**Bear Detective Investigates
Part 1**

Bear poked out his nose through the opening of the chest and looked around. They were in a small room, and the bright sun was shining through the window, bringing a warm glow to everything.

"Eleven fifteen, obviously," Bear said in a serious voice, as he carefully checked the position of the sun.

He looked at Nosey, who was still fast asleep. Bear didn't like to be alone, so he started thinking of some gentle way to wake up his friend. Nosey was not even three years old and usually slept a lot, but Bear decided to give his friend's left ear a little tug, and whispered, "Wake up, sleepyhead. We have a whole house to explore!"

Nosey opened his left eye first and looked at his buddy. He wanted to sleep a bit more, as usual. He obviously had no idea where they were.

"Come on, Nose. We are inside the house. I remember

that you rolled over to my side, but I thought it was just a part of my dream. The people who moved in here must have carried us in."

"Just the way we had planned it..." thought Nosey, and he opened his right eye as well.

"We have tons of things to do," said Bear. "We must find out where exactly we are and who these people are. It may not be safe for us to stay here. Although... it looks pretty good so far, with all these toys..." he grinned, looking around.

He then jumped up as if a bee had stung him.

"Nosey, this couldn't possibly be the warehouse of a toy store, could it?" he asked, looking worried.

Now it was Nosey's turn to be scared. He remembered how difficult it had been for them to escape from the toy store, and how long he had had to wait for Bear to return and get him. That time, he thought he might never see Bear again.

19

His friend returned, and they escaped together, but Nosey still didn't like to think of them possibly being trapped in some sort of a toy store or its warehouse.

"Look Nosey, this looks like a neighbourhood where families live. There are no toy stores or warehouses in these kinds of places."

Nosey wasn't convinced at all, so Bear went on.

"Remember, Nosey, what the real sign of a toy store is?"

Nosey looked at Bear, thinking that this time his friend had really asked a silly question, because of course, the sign of a toy store is tons of toys!

"We are surrounded by tons of toys." Nosey gestured.

"Come on, Nosey, think." Bear was getting happier and happier in the meanwhile, because by now he was quite sure that they were not in a toy store.

Nosey on the other hand just shook his head, insisting that the sign of a toy store was "tons of toys," so Bear had to help.

"Remember Nosey, how many bears and elephants there were in the store?"

This made Nosey's face light up, because he knew exactly what Bear was getting at. He remembered at least two shelves packed with bears, meant to look just like Bear, and there were at least a dozen elephants similar to him. He looked around, and sure enough, he could not see two identical toys. Each one was different!

Bear jumped up and hugged his friend.

"I think we are good. I'll have to do some detective work though..."

So, he pushed up the lid of the chest a bit more to get a better view of the room they were in. His mind started racing as he thought up new plans. He wanted to prove to his friend that they were in a safe place.

Nosey was already organizing the toys around him. He created a special pile for the toys he liked the most, and flew away on the wings of his imagination.

"Let's see... What do detectives need?" and, as he said these words, he imagined himself, Detective Bear McQueen, looking at footprints, collecting clues, taking fingerprints off different objects... He saw himself with a magnifying glass, waving a walking stick and wearing a hat like the great detective, Sherlock Holmes. He adjusted his winter tie with a smile, and said, "I don't really need a hat, but I must have a magnifying glass, a notebook and a pen, a flashlight, a bag for collecting clues, and a fingerprint kit. Let's see... How do I get all these things?" Nosey didn't seem to take much notice. He was still busy sorting toys and was currently admiring a rainbow coloured plastic slinky.

"Let's look for a pen and paper," Bear said, sizing up a few cardboard boxes.

He climbed out of the chest, and, once out, he tossed a few boxes next to each other,

21

creating giant steps so that Nosey could climb in and out easily. Then he started to open boxes, but only found more toys and some books and manuals. There was nothing similar to a notebook or pen or pencil.

"OK, I guess I will have to take mental notes," he thought, but, knowing how forgetful he was, he also knew it wasn't the best idea.

"Let's keep looking... magnifying glass ...." Bear muttered, and he already had a few ideas where to look. He'd come across a microscope set in the second cardboard box. As luck would have it, it came with a great magnifying glass.

"Phew... so far so good. I also need a flashlight, so that I can peek into dark cupboards and corners." And almost as soon as he said it, he found one.

"Let's look for a fingerprint kit now."

He looked everywhere, but couldn't find one so he went back to report his findings to Nosey. He wanted to figure out what to use instead of the fingerprint kit and it helped him to tell all his problems to his friend because as he talked, he often came up with a solution.

"I have to replace the fingerprint kit with something. I guess I could use some soot and white powder and a brush and a tape..."

His friend flapped his ears and pointed with his trunk.

"A Fingerprint Kit!" exclaimed Bear.

"Great job, Nosey!" he said, grinning ear to ear, leaving his friend extremely proud that he could help their common effort by finding something so important.

"Time to get started!" he said and, throwing all his detective gear into a plastic bag, Bear headed towards the door that was slightly open. Nosey watched him with amazement.

Bear looked around and saw a few doors and a staircase leading down to the main floor.

"Down we go!" he said, and started looking for the most exciting way to get downstairs.

Sliding down the railing was too boring. He thought about jumping from one step to the next in a crazy combination of somersaults and cartwheels and screaming his head off, but that didn't seem like such a good idea since he did not have Nosey as an audience.

"I am certainly not going to just walk down the stairs, step by step. Let's see..." Bear was thinking hard.

"I know, I'll race!" he exclaimed, but he soon realized he didn't have anyone to race against. He didn't dare ask Nosey to join him, just in case they had to get back to the room and quickly hide. Bear knew very well that his good friend might get stuck somewhere, or wouldn't be able to jump high enough, or get lost in his daydreams and not be fast enough. This often left a lot of tugging and pulling for Bear.

"But then, who do I race against?" he mumbled.

"I know! It's not a who, it's a what!" he almost yelled out.

He ran back to the room, startling Nosey. He wasn't expecting his friend to be back so soon.

"Nosey, where's the slinky?" Bear asked.

Nosey, who was still sorting the toys, looked up slowly. Bear quickly understood that he had probably just asked Nosey for one of his "favourite" toys.

"I promise to return it," said Bear kindly.

"I just need it to get down the stairs," he added.

And so, Nosey went to his pile of toys and dug out the beautiful rainbow coloured slinky from the very bottom. He handed it over to Bear meaningfully, and he watched his friend disappear again.

Part 2

Bear went to the top of the stairs and threw the plastic bag with the gear down to the spot where he was hoping to land. He then put the slinky at the edge of the top stair, nudged it into starting its spiral down and then hurled himself forward, imitating the slinky. He was summersaulting, head up, head down, alternating every step.

"Whapaty-wham-bim-thump. What a way to have lots of fun!"

He even had time for some mental math as he was bouncing his way down.

"144
    divided
        by
            twelve
                is
                    twelve."

"The slinky won!" he announced as he reached the resting area.

"I just need to focus a bit harder," he said, and he adjusted his winter tie.

"No math this time and I'll win the next round," he said. He started the slinky and jumped.

"Here we go again!"

This time he arrived at his destination before the slinky, feeling very pleased with himself.

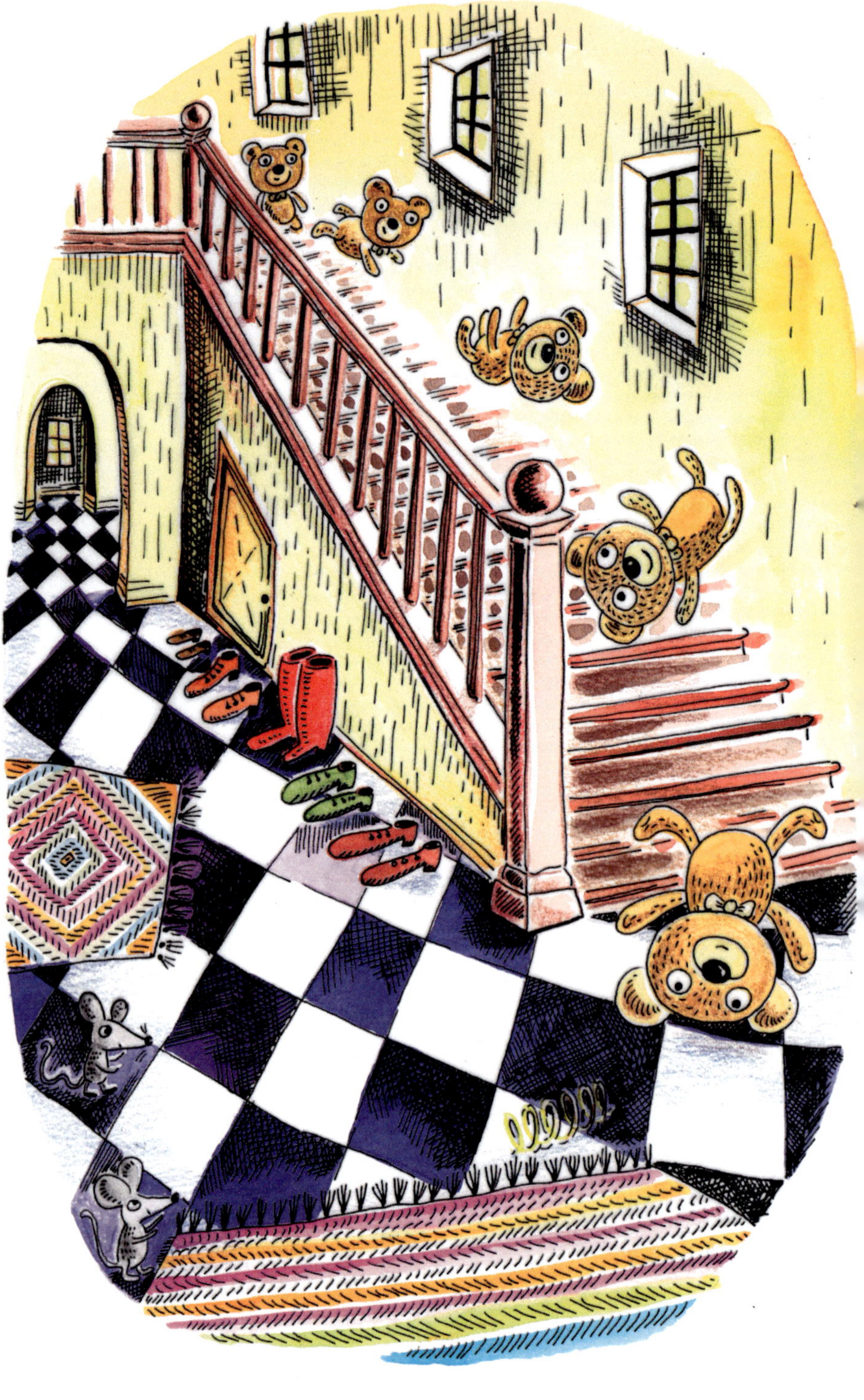

"Now, where was I again?" he thought.

"144 divided by..." and he paused to think.

"I know."

He estimated that there were at least 144 toys in the room upstairs. Based on his toy store experiences, he also figured that a kid gets about 12 toys a year, ranging from Kinder Egg surprises to home-made toys, to bigger toys. This made Bear really scared.

"There may be a twelve-year-old in the house, or... twelve one-year-olds!" he thought, looking alarmed.

Bear didn't continue his thoughts, nor did he bother with getting back to the room in a fun and unusual way. He rushed up as fast as his feet would carry him, and he startled Nosey once again.

"Nosey," he panted, "You must go through all the toys and sort them according to baby toys, toddler toys and toys for bigger kids."

"Okay, I like this," thought Nosey and nodded. "I'm quite the expert at this."

Although he used to be in the baby toy section, he often wandered around at night when no one saw him, and he checked out toys that bigger kids played with.

He flapped his ears, and started his new job immediately.

Bear was relieved that he didn't have to explain to his friend why he gave him this task. They were both afraid of very small kids, especially the ones in strollers, who could tear off an animal's head or ears, just like that. Now, his detective job would be twice as difficult. Not only would he have to check that they were not in a toy store, he would also have to make sure that there were no babies or toddlers living there.

He left his friend behind once again to sort toys and left the room, heading towards the stairs. He jumped up to the top of the railing and slid down fast to continue his detective work.

"Twelve babies or six toddlers." He continued his mental math, and once he was at the bottom of the stairs, he started walking, muttering to himself, without paying too much attention to which way he was going.

He bumped into a closed door and this ended his daydreaming.

"Uh-oh!" he muttered, and stepped back.

"This door must lead down to the basement," he whispered.

"What if there is a little grandma with six very naughty toddlers down there?"

He pressed his right ear flat against the door, but he couldn't hear a thing.

"OK. Let's go on. A good detective collects clues and gets his job done," and saying this he went back towards the stairs, where he had thrown his plastic bag.

"I still need to make sure this is not a toy store or its warehouse."

Bear decided that the spot to the right of the stairs would be his "office." He took out the gear from his plastic bag and got started. Bending slightly forward, equipped with the magnifying glass and a flashlight, he went around following the walls. This way he covered the entire downstairs area. He arrived at his "office" again and summarized his findings.

"I found one hallway, one bathroom, one kitchen, and a dining room and living room. I peeked into the kitchen cabinets and the wardrobe with my flashlight and found no toys or counters for toy displays. I looked at something small that looked like a sugar crystal with my magnifying glass, and it was indeed a sugar crystal. This is clearly a family home. So far so good."

But what about the people who lived there?

"Would they be kind or mean? Did they like honey or jam? Did they have big feet or small feet?" wondered Bear as he decided to look for footprints.

"I wish people were considerate and trampled in mud before they came into the house," he grumbled, scratching his head.

Since there were no footprints, he decided to go back to his "office." He got the fingerprint kit and headed towards the kitchen. "I know just what I will do. I will take the fingerprints off the pots and pans, to compare them with the fingerprints on the toys. If the prints on the toys are the same as the ones on the pots, then the people who live here are the ones playing with the toys. The prints on the pots must be adult prints, because no small kid would be allowed to cook at a stove. This will be fun!"

He walked through kitchen utensils, fruit and vegetables, sailed across the sink in a bowl using a wooden spoon for a paddle and he eventually arrived at the stove. He chose the lid of the biggest pot and carefully took out his fingerprint kit. He sprinkled white powder on the lid and gently brushed it away with the brush. Now he could see that the lid was full of fingerprints. Very pleased, he took out the tape from the kit, and lifted off a few beautiful prints.

Just then, he heard a car door slam.

"Uh-oh! What if they're coming home?"

He had just enough time to pack up everything when he spotted two people through the kitchen window approaching the front door.

"That's it. I'll never have time to get upstairs. Hide, quick!" he said to himself, and with this he jumped into a drawer.

He waited in the dark, not daring to move, listening for sounds, but he didn't hear a thing.

"Where could they have disappeared to?" he wondered. He realized shortly that they must have been the neighbours.

Thinking that it was probably safe to come out, he did so, but he decided to end his detective adventure for today because it was getting dark and people were returning home. He raced back to his office and, on the way, he just threw any loose object that he came across into his plastic bag.

He heard another car door slam, and then another...

"I'd better run." He dashed up the stairs as fast as he could. He was almost upstairs when he remembered Nosey's slinky.

"Oh, no! Where did I leave it?" He rushed back down,

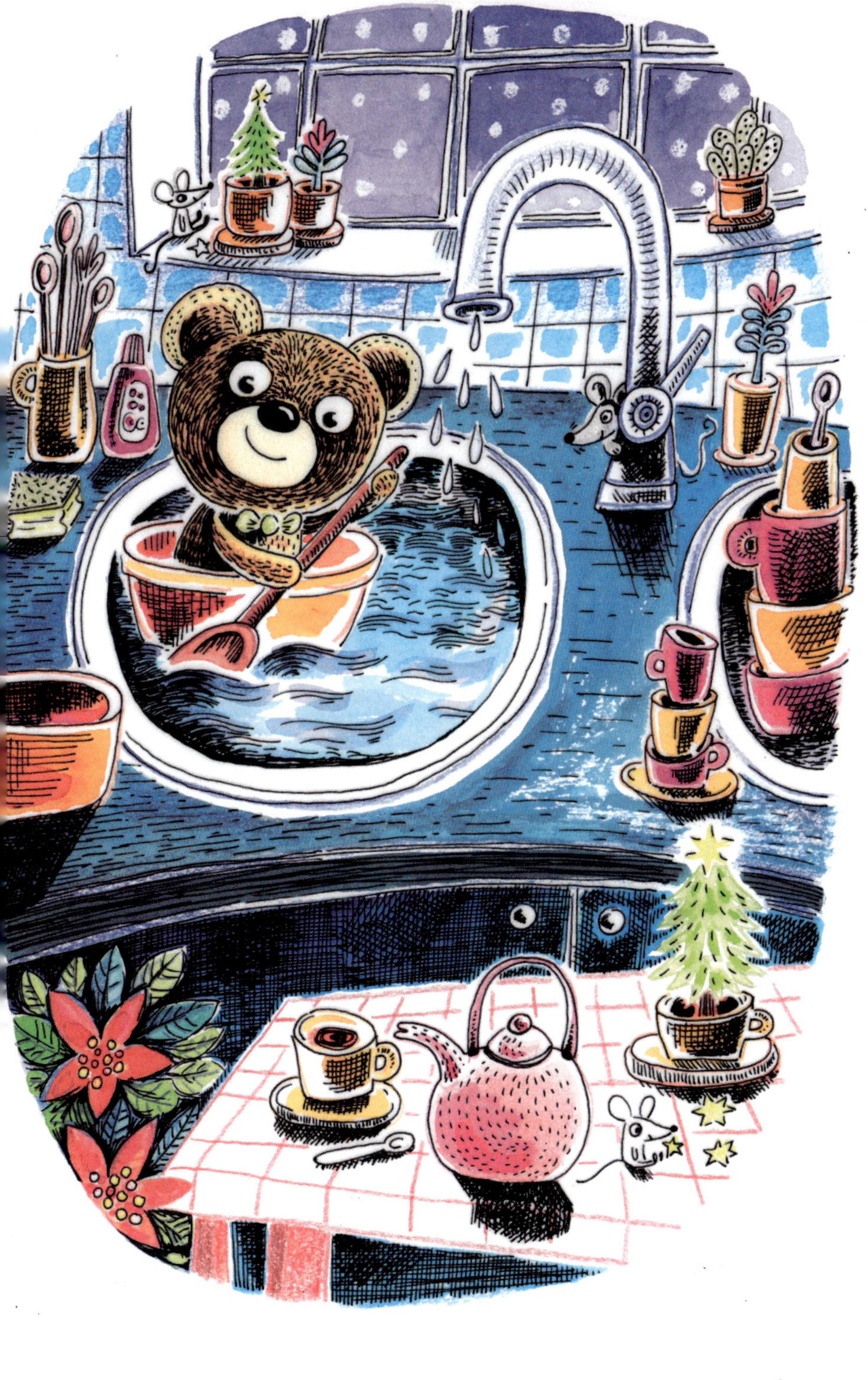

thinking as hard as he could. Luckily, he found the slinky at the bottom of the stairs, so he could run back up again quickly. He was just at the resting point when he heard the click of a key.

"Uh-oh! This time it's not the neighbours." Bear was scared. "What if I get caught?"

...And then he had a brilliant idea. He threw one end of the slinky up the railing, while he hung on to the other end. As the slinky got caught in the rails, Bear was pulled up instantly to the second floor.

The footsteps were already on the stairs when Bear entered the room where Nosey had been waiting. He was a bit shaky.

"Quick Nosey, hide. They're home."

The two animals disappeared into the very bottom of the chest and stayed close to each other, hoping that no one would enter the room and discover them.

They heard noises for a while: people going up and down stairs, the faraway sounds of a TV, but no one entered the room they were in.

"I didn't have enough time to collect all the clues I wanted to," Bear whispered to his friend. "I did get some fingerprints, though," he added smiling, "and there is some other stuff in the plastic bag. We'll have to check everything out when we're alone, again. I couldn't even find where they keep their honey... Anyway, the main thing is that we are NOT in a toy store."

This made Nosey very happy.

The animals snuggled together, and Bear knew that

Nosey would soon fall asleep. It was dark outside, and Nosey was already dreaming a sweet dream about a secret plan he hatched after his friend had told him that he couldn't find the honey.

Bear stayed awake for a while, listening for noises, ready to protect his friend, if necessary, but no one disturbed the animals. Eventually, the whole house was cloaked in silence, and so Bear climbed out of the chest quietly and up onto the windowsill. It seemed as though a new star lit up in the sky with each new passing moment. Bear watched the silent light show with a twinkle of amazement in his otherwise mischievous eyes. He recognized the Little Dipper, his favourite, and then held his breath as he spotted what seemed to be a moving star.

"An airplane," he whispered slowly, and he thought of his own dear old plane they had had to leave behind at the airport. He was a little sad, but grinned at the thought of moving in with an airplane. Christmas was just around the corner, and he couldn't help thinking of a family, a loving, caring family, where he would always be the star attraction, where he would have a chance to do all the mischievous tricks a bear could ever dream up, and he would entertain his masters, and pull their legs, day in and day out. He would never stop laughing and jumping and laughing and just having the most unimaginable fun time a bear and his elephant friend could possibly have in a family.

Forever.

Chapter Three

**Nosey is Lost!
Part 1**

Nosey turned over on his right side in his sleep and felt the sharp tip of a small spinning top push against his plump belly. He opened his left eye slowly.

"Aha. My new alarm clock invention works," he said to himself, with a sleepy, but very satisfied smile.

Nosey tried to imitate his friend. Whenever Bear came up with a new invention, Nosey tried to think up something new as well, but many of his ideas were left undiscovered. He either forgot about them by the time he woke up in the morning, or he went on and on perfecting an idea for ages, in secret.

This time, he invented the silent alarm clock. You see, when two people sleep in the same room, but only one of them needs to wake up, one obviously doesn't want to disturb the other person. Nosey realized that he turns over from his left side to his right each night, so if he planted a "silent alarm clock" to his right, he would wake up when he rolled over.

And so, he did. He felt the tip of the top, and woke up without waking Bear.

Just as he had expected.

Feeling very satisfied with himself, he opened his right eye too, and sat up. He had a secret plan to carry out. He would sneak down during the night and find out where the honey was kept. Bear didn't have time to do this because the people returned unexpectedly and he had to race back to their hiding spot. Nosey would continue the mission and surprise Bear, first thing in the morning with the good news.

"Aha! That'll be something," he thought, his eyes shining with joy in the little room lit by stars. But first, he had to make a plan. Nosey remembered every detail of Bear's plan when he was getting ready for his detective mission.

"Well, an elephant never..." and he stopped in mid sentence, because he'd lost his train of thought. He shook his head slightly.

"Oh well," he sighed. "I forgot it. Better go on." But saying this, he jumped up, because now he remembered: "An elephant never forgets."

"I knew that," he thought with a big smile, feeling that special elephant power, instantly. He went on with his plans.

"I definitely need a flashlight because it's really dark," he thought.

"And the slinky," he added, as he clearly remembered

how Bear appeared completely out of nowhere to borrow his beautiful rainbow coloured slinky, "to get down the stairs."

"That should be it," Nosey thought, but he felt that something was missing.

Of course, a toy. He never left for longer periods without one. He decided to take the bubble blowing bottle. He climbed out of the chest without making a sound and stood in the dim moonlight outside the chest, next to two oversized red boxing gloves. He didn't dare turn on his flashlight. Luckily, the light of the crescent moon gave him just enough light to see. He carefully removed the bubble blowing bottle from under the right glove and felt around for the slinky. He knew exactly where to find it, so he soon had everything he needed: the flashlight, the slinky and the bubble blowing bottle.

"All set," he thought, and he was pretty sure Bear would have agreed. He went to the half-shut door and snuck out. Once outside the room, he found himself in complete darkness and turned on the flashlight. He saw three doors around him, all closed, and a flight of stairs leading down.

"That's where I'll have

to use the slinky," he muttered, "But how exactly do I use this to get down?" he wondered, looking at the slinky.

"If I were a long and very skinny elephant, I could get inside it, and as it climbs down the stairs, I could be transported down as a passenger. But..." and here he paused for a bit, and looked proudly at his plump belly "I am not a long and skinny Elephant."

While he was thinking, he was turning the slinky around, pulling it onto his nose, stepping into it with one leg and then the other, and wrapping it around himself like a shawl. He connected one end to his right leg and then to his left and the other end to his nose. In that very moment he lost his balance. He tripped and went rolling down the stairs: a big Nosey and slinky entanglement rolling and rolling endlessly until he found himself at the very bottom of the two flights.

It was sheer luck that the bubble blowing bottle and the flashlight were also caught in the entanglement, so finally, the entire Honey Discovery Team was lying at the bottom of the stairs, with Nosey half unconscious.

When he came to, he freed his two feet that were stuck

in the slinky and pulled his trunk out of a few rainbow-colored loops. He looked up the stairs, and mumbled, completely puzzled:

"I don't get this. Why would Bear have decided to go through all this trouble just to get down the stairs? Bears do really weird things sometimes," he sighed, thinking of his good friend and all the strange things he had seen him do. This made him happy, so he grinned as he looked around in the dark.

"Let's see...where do these people keep their honey...?" he wondered.

"In all the picture books I have seen so far, the honey is always next to the strawberry jam in the kitchen. If I find the kitchen and then the strawberry jam, I'll find the honey," concluded Nosey, and he checked his surroundings with his flashlight. He was in the dining room. He turned to his right and spotted a red pail and mop in a distant corner.

"Aha! That's it!" and he galloped towards the pail and mop, flapping his ears, cheerfully.

He looked around in the kitchen and saw some cabinets above the counter.

"That's where I'll find the strawberry jam. I'll just have to jump up!"

Bear and Nosey measured how high they could jump each and every day. Nosey knew very well that he couldn't have jumped high enough to reach the counter a few days ago, but he decided to try because he was growing and developing. One day he might be able to do something

39

he couldn't do the previous day. That's what Bear always told him, and he never doubted Bear.

Nosey jumped up and fell back to the same spot from where he'd started.

"I still can't jump high enough. I'm still developing," he sighed, and began searching for a better solution, just like Bear would have.

He looked at the four drawers that were under the counter and he had an idea. He pulled out the bottom drawer, hopped on the rim, then pulled out the next drawer and hopped up again, until he created a staircase with all four drawers pulled out and...

"Ta-dah!" He was on the countertop. It was like an obstacle course, full of all kinds of kitchen utensils and gadgets. He saw a cabinet door half ajar above the sink with some bottles.

"Strawberry jam," and he headed towards the sink, pushing aside whatever got in his way: the toaster oven, a coffee-making machine and three cookie jars. He reached the sink that was sitting there all empty. He thought for a moment and then went back a few steps. He disappeared behind two giant cereal boxes and reappeared pulling a cutting board behind him that was almost as big as he was.

He was going to lay it down as a bridge. Nosey enjoyed hauling wood because it reminded him of his real ancestors, mighty beasts of burden, who moved enormous logs around all day in countries like India and Thailand.

Of course, Nosey wouldn't have liked to haul wood day

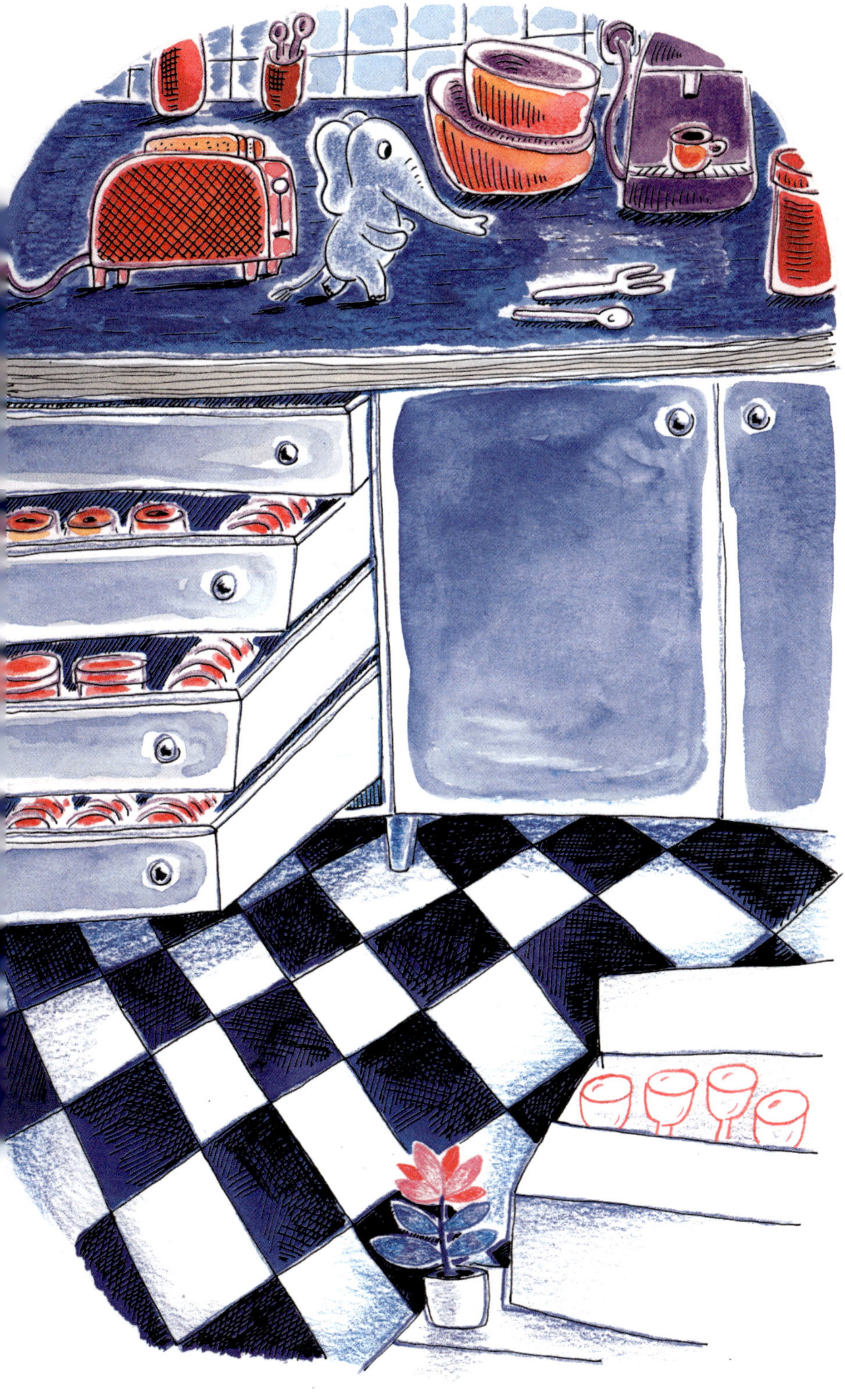

and night because he preferred to play. Hauling this wood was just like a game to him.

He started walking across his newly constructed "bridge" comfortably. When he reached the middle, he decided to play circus elephant. As the moon shone through the kitchen window, he imagined that he was in the centre of the spotlight. He could almost hear the applause of the audience, so he lifted one leg and bowed. And that did it. He lost his balance and went tumbling down to the kitchen floor.

"Here we go again." But just as he was about to climb back onto the counter, he heard noises coming from the direction of the living room. Some mechanism was at work. Nosey could hear springs creaking, and then a shrill

"Cuckoo! Cuckoo! Cuckoo! Cuckoo!"

"A cuckoo clock!" thought Nosey cheerfully, feeling the comfort of having company. He liked cuckoo clocks, so he went to check it out. He flashed around with his flashlight, but couldn't see the clock anywhere.

"Where could this cuckoo be hiding?" he wondered, pointing his flashlight to all corners of the living room carefully. He then jumped with surprise because what he saw on top of the coffee table was none other than

A Jar of Honey!

He was absolutely overjoyed. Finally, he could tell Bear where the honey was kept and his friend would be very proud of him. He climbed up onto the sofa and landed on the table with an easy jump. He saw a pipe on some newspaper next to the jar of honey.

"Honey and a bubble blowing pipe?" Nosey asked himself with surprise. He had never seen a real wooden pipe before. He was sure that the pipe-shaped object was used for blowing bubbles.

"I must try it with my bubble blowing stuff," he said, and filled up the pipe carefully with bubble-blowing liquid. He created tons and tons of beautiful bubbles, big and small, individual ones and clusters, until Nosey was completely surrounded by them. They were bouncing around him playfully, shimmering in the starlit room. He started playing with them. First, he bounced them gently around with his trunk, pretending to be a juggler, he then fanned the whimsical creations around with his ears. He even tried to have them land in certain spots. He got more and more carried away, moving faster and faster, until his beautiful improvisation turned into a kind of funny, wild dance.

Unexpectedly, with one swift gesture he sent the jar of honey flying. It landed with a big thump on the carpet, ending Nosey's show.

"Uh-oh!" and he wished he knew what to do next. He was sitting on top of the coffee table, sadly looking at the last bubble as it landed on the green pillow on the couch.

"What if I woke up the people? Oh no! Better hide." he whispered.

And with this, Nosey jumped onto the sofa and hid behind the green pillow, trying to make himself as small as he could. He was frightened.

Part 2

Bear woke up as if a bee had stung him. He sat up in the chest with both eyes wide open. The noise from downstairs had woken him up. He poked around to his right where Nosey had been sleeping and grabbed at something furry, but he realized it was less than half the size of his friend.

"It must be that silly furry duck!" he said to himself. "Where is Nosey?"

He poked around a bit further, but Nosey was nowhere.

"He's wandered off again," Bear said, terrified.

"How am I going to find him in the dark? And what if he makes some noise and the people wake up and they end up finding him?" Bear was in a panic. He remembered very well how Nosey used to wander off at night in the toy store. A salesperson usually found him in the morning, playing with LEGO toys or reading a picture book.

"These kids!" they would hear. "They should know better than picking up toys and dropping them off where they please."

Nosey was always carried back carefully to his department and placed back on the shelf with the other elephants. But what if someone finds him and does not put him back into the chest, because they don't even know he lives there, and instead, he is given to some baby or gets thrown out?

Bear was looking for the flashlight and climbing out of the chest at the same time. However, the flashlight was not where he had left it.

"Nosey took the flashlight!" Bear said, almost whining. "Now what do I do?"

He looked out of the window and saw that the sky was clear. There were a million stars to help him and the moon was trying to grow as well. Unfortunately, it was still just a sliver of a crescent.

Bear hurried to the door carefully, and snuck out.

"Well, I hope Nosey is somewhere here," he said to himself, arriving at the bottom of the stairs.

"Nosey, Nose! Where are you?" he whispered.

Nosey was just about to make a big, happy appearance from behind the green pillow when a door was thrown open upstairs, and all the lights were turned on.

"Uh-oh!" Bear looked around panic-stricken, and he had just enough time to hide inside a red backpack that was on the floor near the dining room table.

Footsteps were heard coming down the stairs. Nosey was wagging his tail in fear behind the green pillow, and Bear, with no tail to wag, just wriggled his muzzle at top speed, scared out of his rags.

"Well, well," they heard a guy's voice.

"It seems like we have a bear in this house and he is after my honey!"

On hearing this, Bear froze.

In reality, the young man had no idea how the jar of honey landed on the carpet. He picked up his pipe and realized it was covered in soap.

"Hmmm, what happened to my pipe?" he asked himself, thoroughly puzzled. For a split second he saw the image of his wife Hanna blowing bubbles with his pipe in the middle of the night and chuckled. He then saw her red backpack lying on the floor, so he picked it up and put it on one of the dining room chairs. Bear held his breath and peeked out.

"Mighty whiskers, I can't see anything from here." he said to himself. He wasn't very happy with his new position.

The guy sat down on the sofa and leaned against the green pillow as he yawned.

"Why is this pillow so lumpy?" he asked out loud, and was just about to plump up the pillow and reveal Nosey's hiding place, when a second voice was heard from upstairs. "Phil, what was that noise?" Hanna asked.

"A bear, I guess" Phil chuckled.

Lighter footsteps were heard coming down the stairs approaching the living room.

"What did you say it was?" she asked with a sleepy smile and ruffled hair.

"A bear, of course. Look, he was after the honey I was going to use to prepare my pipe!" he said.

Trapped in the backpack, Bear would have definitely liked to disappear off the face of the Earth at this point.

"Aha," she said, "a bear. Well, as long as it has some manners and it isn't bigger than a cat, I'm fine with it." She headed towards the kitchen where she noticed the open drawers and the cutting board across the sink.

"Phil, were you looking for something?"

"No, why are you asking?" and he went out to the kitchen too.

Bear was waiting for this moment ever since he was put on the chair.

He jumped off the chair with the red backpack still over his head, and using it as cover, he scurried towards the fireplace because he thought he had seen something grey just between the fireplace and the TV.

"Nosey, Nose!" he whispered.

Nosey peeked out from behind the green pillow but didn't see Bear, because, of course, Bear was concealed inside the red backpack. Bear couldn't see Nosey either because he was covered by the green pillow.

Footsteps were nearing again, so Nosey decided to jump. He landed behind the sofa, next to a familiar object: the yellow plastic bucket.

"A perfect hiding place," thought Nosey and dived into the bucket right away. It only took a split second for him to realize that he was completely stuck, upside down.

In the meantime, Phil was out of eyesight somewhere at the entrance door, so Bear could continue his search. He looked behind the curtains and lifted everything that he came across and could be lifted.

Nosey was nowhere to be found.

He spotted a laundry basket.

"Shaped like an elephant?" he muttered and charged towards it, beginning to feel slightly desperate. He jumped out of the red backpack and dived right in.

Just as he started searching for Nosey, he heard footsteps coming and the female voice saying: "Could you take that laundry basket up please, Phil?"

"Mighty Polar Bear!" Bear exclaimed, as he felt himself being lifted. Not wasting a second, he wrapped himself into a towel and jumped out of the basket, landing on the dining room carpet. Phil carried the basket upstairs without noticing a thing.

Bear stayed wrapped in the towel, looking like a very hairy lady with a shawl around her head. He headed towards the living room. While this had been going on, Nosey had been making his way out from behind the sofa, bucket on his head, right side up. He had been inching ahead, completely lost. Finally, exhausted, he sat down.

Bear was also moving ahead still disguised. He was almost at the curtains, when footsteps were heard from upstairs.

"Oh, no! He'll notice the towel and he'll get me." Bear whimpered, so he threw the towel behind him and looked for the nearest hiding spot. It happened to be an old hat box.

Bear jumped out of his cover and into the hatbox just to see a glimpse

50

of a yellow bucket from the corner of his eyes. Already safe in the hatbox, Bear realized that there was something wrong with what he had seen. The bucket was upside down, hovering about 20 centimeters above the ground and kind of wobbling, just as if...

"Oh my! Nosey! It's got to be him!"

Bear wasn't sure if he should be overjoyed or scared to death. He tried to peek out again, but he couldn't see a thing.

"I must move," he decided.

He first put the hatbox on his head, upside down, and took a few steps. This clearly did not work. He had no idea where he was going, so he tipped the hatbox to the side and rolled ahead by walking inside the box. This was much better, because he could move faster and it was easier to peek out.

Out of nowhere, Bear noticed something that would have scared even the mightiest grizzly. Two enormous feet were planted right next to the hatbox, and the feet were attached to a full-sized person. The voice belonging to the feet said, "I didn't notice dropping this towel...

strange..." and to Bear's relief the person moved away to pick it up and headed upstairs to put it with the rest of the laundry.

When he returned, everything started happening simultaneously.

Phil tripped over the hatbox, and he slid headfirst right into the kitchen. Hanna started screaming. Bear decided to give up his cover, and was dismayed to see Nosey marching right down the middle of the living room towards the kitchen chaos: bucket on his head, right foot dragging along a fishing line. The line was attached to a fishing rod that was lying a jump away from Bear.

And here, Knox Ursus Horribilis McQueen, jumped into action. He almost flew over to the fishing rod, and reeled Nosey back to safety. He gave him a quick hug coupled with a firm push that directed him behind the curtains. There, Bear removed the bucket from his head, and Nosey just stood there, trying to figure out what exactly had happened to him, but definitely feeling a whole lot like crying...with relief.

Bear looked at him and before he said anything, he peeked out from behind the curtains to see if the couple was still in the kitchen. They were. However, Bear also saw something that choked him up a bit. He saw a golden streak of honey leading from the honey jar that was lying on the carpet, towards Nosey's bubble-blowing bottle that was right next to it.

Bear realized that his friend was trying to find the honey for him, so he just hugged him, and said, "Thank you, Nosey."

Faint noises could be heard from the kitchen.

"Are you sure, you're OK?" she asked.

"Of course, I am. I have no idea though how that hatbox got right under my feet..."

"Well, I hope this was not a warm-up for tomorrow's ice-skating. Will you be OK to skate?" she asked.

"Oh yeah, no big deal. I really didn't hurt myself."

"That's great, because I'm really looking forward to tomorrow. I've already packed the blue duffle bag."

"Let's try to get some sleep. What a weird night this has been!" he said, getting up.

The animals heard the couple going upstairs. The lights were turned off, and the whole house was quiet once again.

Bear looked at Nosey, and saw that his friend was on the verge of falling asleep.

"We need to go back to the treasure chest." Bear whispered.

Nosey produced the flashlight from out of nowhere, waved his left ear, and he fell asleep on the spot. Bear sat next to him, thinking for a few minutes, but of course he was mighty exhausted as well. He peeked out from behind the curtains, flashed around with the flashlight and saw the blue duffle bag. A big smile appeared on his muzzle. This time, he had a secret plan. He gently pushed his friend towards the bag. Turning the bag sideways, he rolled Nosey in, and then followed him. He covered Nosey and then himself with sweaters he found in the bag.

Bear thought of one of their favourite toys from the toy store: a miniature ice rink. Guided by invisible magnets, tiny figures twirled and swirled as they skated happily to Jingle Bells. Around the rink, there were some pine trees and a few benches. A dog was sitting next to the bench. Bear was soon dreaming about a glimmering ice rink and a beautiful bonfire. He too, was twirling and swirling under the moonlight, drawing myriads of loops on the ice.

Chapter Four

**Skating under the Stars
Part 1**

It was past noon, and the sun had trouble peeking out from behind the clouds. Everything was wrapped in a thick, grey, wintry fog.

Bear woke up at the bottom of the duffle bag. He pushed his small nose upwards, nudging a skate out of his way, and inched ahead very carefully. He rustled a plastic bag accidentally, so he stopped to listen if anyone had heard him. There was a deep silence. He moved ahead in another direction. He soon stuck his head out of the bag.

"Wow, we're in the car already!" he said, observing the view from the back seat. The duffle bag was placed on top of another bag so he could see the entrance of the house they had moved into three days ago. He smiled as he recognized the tree where they had been practicing their meowing. The big cat was sitting in front of the same door, ready for its meowing routine.

"I still think I can meow better than you," giggled Bear, remembering how hard he had worked to produce a convincing meow, so they could get into a house.

He looked around inside the car, and noticed that at the end of the duffle bag, Nosey's big furry trunk was sticking out like some abandoned periscope: a kind of crooked, hairy periscope. His friend was still asleep. Bear crept up to him and gently pushed his trunk back in. He decided to stand guard, but he didn't want to be fully exposed, so he looked for a disguise. Luckily, it was winter, so there were all kinds of hats and shawls on the back seat. Bear rummaged through and found just what he was looking for: a balaclava.

"Tee-hee," he giggled, ready for fun.

"I like this," he said and he disappeared inside the balaclava and started looking for the eye slot. His mischievous eyes soon appeared, and he looked right and left. He had to keep an eye on the door. Just then, it flung wide open.

"Oops, here they come," and without a thought, he dived into the middle of the duffle bag. He felt a soft nudge on the right side of his belly. Bear searched for his peeking-hole and saw Nosey, who had been patiently digging his way through the contents of the duffle bag trying to find him.

"Nosey, it's me, here!" Bear whispered, and not realizing how funny he looked, he made his friend laugh and jump so hard it made the duffle bag shake.

"Stop that Nosey," he said, and the more serious he tried to be, the more hilarious he looked.

"They just came out of the house."

"You hide and I'll keep watch," said Bear, the organizer. Nosey, feeling a little sad that it wasn't fun-time yet, disappeared among the sweaters.

"Now, back to work. Where are these people?" he wondered, and immediately wished he hadn't, because they were standing right outside the car, about to get in.

"Mighty grizzly paws!" Bear gasped, and he dived back into the bag. In no time at all, he was in a safe spot, with Nosey next to him. They were waiting in tense excitement. Would this be fun, or had they managed to get themselves into a whole heap of trouble? Bear decided to take a risk yesterday, but now he wasn't so sure he should have.

"Oh, well," he sighed, "people don't eat rag animals." and he paused.

"If we get into trouble, we just have to get out of it," concluded the little brown furry creature with devilishly twinkling greenish-brown eyes.

"Couldn't be that bad going skating," he said to Nosey.

Nosey had no idea why he was in the duffle bag, nor did he have any knowledge of Bear's plans. He was just beginning to realize all this.

"I'll tell you what's going on," Bear said and hugged his friend. He went very close to his right ear, and made a funnel out of it so that he could whisper without anyone else hearing. When Bear finished, Nosey sat as still as a statue, with joy in his eyes.

They were going skating!

Right then, the car engine started up and they were on their way.

The car stopped after fifteen minutes. First, they heard one door slam, then the other. They could be taken out of the car to go skating any second. A few minutes passed, but there was no movement and not a single sound to be heard.

"How can they skate without skates?" complained Bear, looking at the skates that were still in the duffle bag.

"I have to check this out. Nosey," he said, turning to his friend. "Could you come closer to the surface please? I may need your help." Bear had no idea what exactly his friend would help him with, but it was always good to have him nearby. The animals poked their heads out. They were alone in the car.

"I must get out to see what this is all about," said Bear.

"We're in a locked car," Nosey warned pointing at the doors.

"I can see that Nose, but there must be a way to get out. Let's see..." and he got the balaclava off and yelled out, "The window!" and he did not pay too much attention to his friend, who was shaking his head in disbelief, "All the windows are closed."

"Nosey, let's examine that window. I think it is a traditional knob on the handle type that you have to turn clockwise to lower. If they have power windows, we're in trouble." Nosey sighed and just wished they could wait patiently until the couple got back. But then again, he was excited to see how Bear would open the window, so he offered to help his friend.

"Thanks, Nose," Bear said gratefully.

"I saw a fanny pack in the blue duffle bag. We will need that and some smaller things that weigh only as much as we can carry," said the inventor in action.

While Bear sat facing the knob that was exactly at the eleven o'clock position, Nosey got the fanny pack and started bringing cans of Coke he had found.

"That's exactly what we need. You see, to open the window, we have to turn the handle clockwise. If we adjust the strap of the fanny pack like this, we can hang it on the knob just like that! All we have to do is pack cans of Coke into it one after the other. Eventually the weight of the Coke will pull the handle down to the six o'clock position. Then I can climb out," said Bear, hardly able to contain his excitement.

The animals started putting the Cokes in, one by one, and already after the second can, the handle moved. After three Cokes, the handle slid down obediently to the six o'clock position.

"We made it!" screamed Bear, and he saw that there was just enough space to squeeze himself through the narrow opening.

Nosey would have loved to talk his friend out of leaving the car, but knowing how stubborn he was, he decided to grab a shoelace and tie one end to Bear's paw while he hung on to the other end. Bear didn't protest, and Nosey was very relieved. He could pull his friend back into the car in case of an emergency.

"OK Nosey, here I ... go-o-o-oh..."

Part 2

Bear landed on soft fresh snow and adjusted his winter tie. He hardly even had time to glance around, when he heard a very kind, deep voice.

"Hey, a bear!" the voice said, and as Bear looked up, he saw a generous, suntanned face, with a pair of the kindest, most mischievous green eyes. They were getting closer and closer to him.

"Come to Papa. There," he said, as he bent down and lifted Bear up.

Nosey heard some noises and the shoelace was instantly jerked out of his grasp. He tried to jump after it and grab on to the disappearing end with his trunk, but it slipped away and disappeared through the window.

"Oh no!" Nosey cried out. "What am I going to do?" He was so scared that the whole world seemed to be spinning with him at top speed. He heard voices outside the car and realized he had to fight his fear and help his friend. He climbed on top of the duffle bag and what he saw scared him more than ever.

Bear was in the hands of a stranger. Nosey went into a panic. What if this stranger takes Bear away? He knew he had to come up with an idea and fast.

"I can't fit through that small opening," he said with disappointment.

"So, I can't go after Bear," he thought, getting more desperate, because he knew he only had seconds to act.

"If I threw a can of Coke through the window, and it fell on this guy's foot, he would faint and drop Bear. Then Bear would be free and I could help him get back into the car," thought Nosey.

In the meantime, Bear didn't know whether to be scared or amused.

"Lucky I came by, or you would have gotten soaking wet," the stranger said, dusting the snow off Bear, carefully. He was about to go on about how dangerous it was to catch a cold just before Christmas, when he erupted into laughter.

"A Bear on a leash. That's just like Phil. Didn't know he had a bear. I guess he was going to introduce you to me next week," he said happily, examining Bear from all angles, and making sure that not a single flake of snow was left on him.

"Great guy that Phil is. Kinda' crazy, but definitely great. You shouldn't wander away from him, you know."

And with these words, Jimmy reached into the car through the window to open the door. He placed Bear gently back on the back seat, and said, "Merry Christmas, bear!"

He slammed the door shut and left oversized footprints

in the snow as he disappeared with his red snow shovel in the direction of Tim Horton's.

Fluffy and fresh snowflakes started falling again.

Bear sat on the car seat for a moment, trying to figure out if it was good or bad that he was back exactly where he had started, only half noticing Nosey who was so happy that he improvised the wildest victory dance with the most ear-flapping, jumping and tail-wagging ever seen or performed by a rag elephant.

Bear eventually realized that Nosey thought that he had been in great danger, so he told him about every detail of his short adventure.

"That was a nice guy. Sorry that I scared you, Nosey!" and saying this, he fell back into his thoughts again.

"Nosey, let's go after this guy and find out if he wants to adopt us," Bear finally blurted out.

However, by the time Bear climbed on top of the duffle bag, Jimmy, and his red shovel, had completely disappeared from sight, as if the snow had swallowed him up.

"Oh well, it was nice meeting him, but I bet he doesn't have a treasure chest or skates like Phil and Hanna..." Bear rambled on.

As he was talking to Nosey, Bear realized that he wasn't really paying attention to what he was saying, because all he could hear echoing in his rag head was, "Great guy that Phil is. Kinda' crazy but definitely great. You shouldn't wander away from him."

Both "great" and "crazy" sounded good to Bear, because he secretly liked to think of himself, too, as great and crazy.

For a while Bear watched the snowflakes as they drifted by playfully. He then turned to Nosey and said: "Nosey, I think we found a great and most importantly, a crazy guy, and Hanna can't be that bad either, so we probably won't have to move out."

Right then, they heard car keys click in the lock, so they did the obvious: both animals disappeared in the duffle bag in an instant.

Phil and Hanna sat in the car and Bear could only hear snippets of what they said. Phil mentioned "turkey" several times, but neither "skates" nor "skating" came up in their conversation.

"Nosey, these guys are never going to take us skating if it goes on like this," complained Bear.

The car engine started up again and the animals were fairly certain that they were on their way to a turkey farm. In just a few minutes the car stopped and they could hear two doors slam. Nosey was keeping his paws crossed that Bear would not want to leave him in the car again, and, as if Bear had read his friend's thoughts, he said, "I'm not going to wander off. I'll stay in the car but I want to peek out to see where we are. Then we'll wait patiently for these guys to return and take us skating."

Nosey couldn't believe his mighty ears. He wanted to thank Bear, so he untied the shoelace from Bear's paw.

"Thanks, Nosey! Just going to the front. Be back sooner than you could sneeze," said Bear, and he disappeared, leaving a rather worried Nosey behind, who was just realizing he couldn't sneeze and he had no idea how long it takes. He decided to teach himself the mysterious art of sneezing. He sniffed at different objects, but he wasn't making much progress. He was just about to poke his trunk into a coffee mug when he saw Bear return.

"This is some kind of a Christmas brunch place. People come here to stuff themselves with breakfast and lunch at the same time. I guess they eat a few turkeys and then go home. Or skating, I hope," sighed Bear.

"OK, Nosey, let's see, what do we know about skating anyway?"

The idea of skating excited Bear tremendously, but he was as cool as a polar bear, and he started racking his brain for things he had heard or read about skating.

"Do you know that in Ottawa, the capital of Canada, lots of people skate on the Rideau Canal in winter, eating beaver tails while they skate? I read this in a book once."

Nosey shook his head and poked Bear to show him he didn't believe this at all. He was positive that there was no way people could skate with big furry beavers or even just their tails hanging out of their mouths.

"Silly Nosey, beaver tails are a delicious kind of pastry made from flour and sugar with lots of cinnamon. You'd love it! I know I would."

"That sounds much better," he winked at Bear.

As they chatted on and on, they heard noises again, but this time they didn't have to dive, because they were already inside the duffle bag.

"It has to be happening now. We're going skating" they both thought.

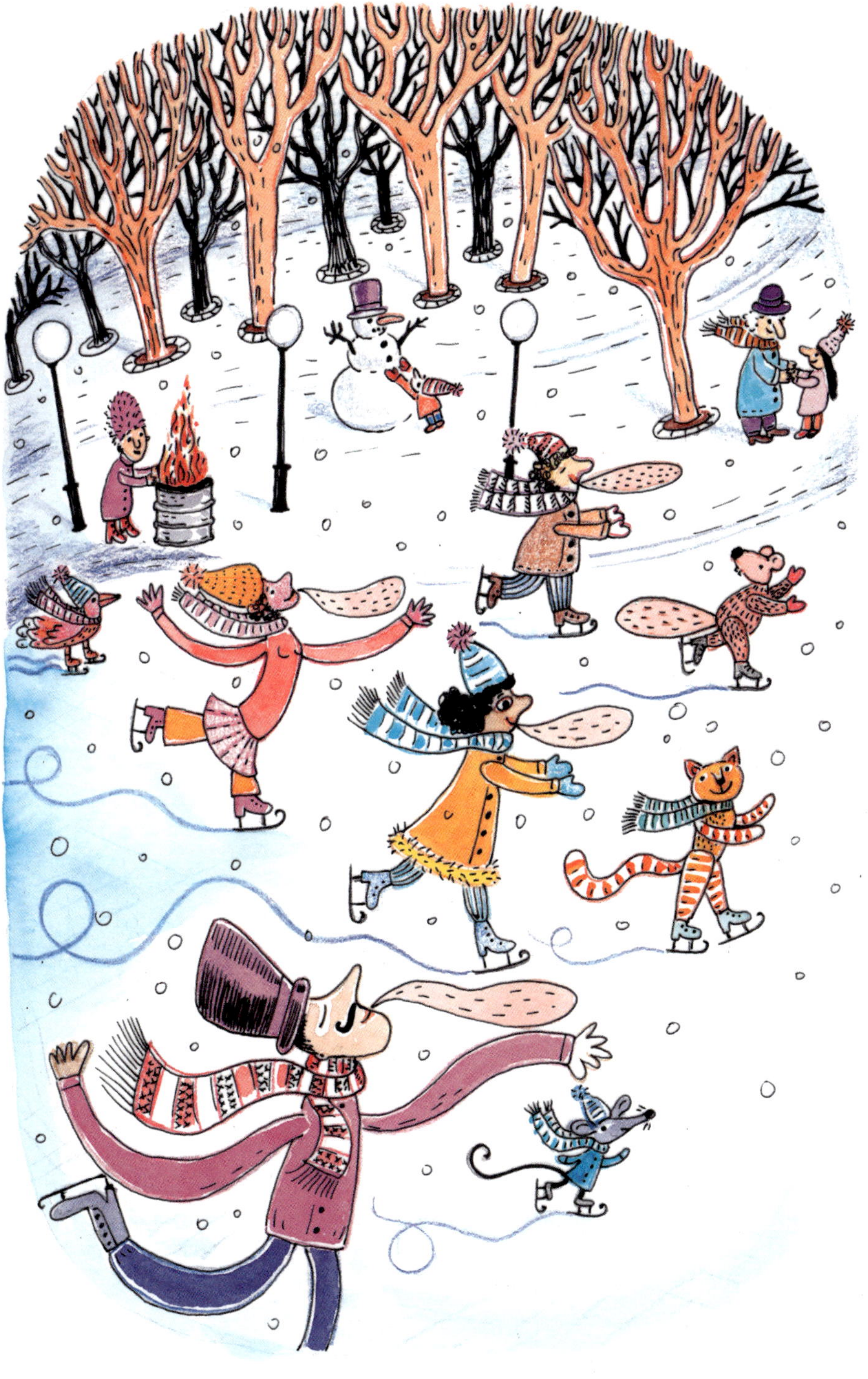

The engine started up and they drove for quite a while. Almost half an hour passed. The animals did not gossip or fidget. They waited with great anticipation for the big moment to arrive.

Finally, the car stopped and there was quite a commotion. Hands poked into the duffle bag, and they could hear things like "Did you get the shawl?" and then "What on earth happened to these shoelaces? Why are they not in the skates?" and the poking and the commotion continued. Bear felt a hand right on his belly once, but the target was an earmuff, not him. Both animals were expecting that any moment, the bag would finally be taken out of the car. They waited and waited, until one pair of skates was removed, then the other. They could hear car doors slam and then, silence.

They both wanted to scream: "It's not fair! You must take us skating too!" But they didn't scream. They were just terribly disappointed.

"Look Nosey," said Bear breaking the silence. Let's climb out and check if we can see the rink from here."

The animals climbed out slowly while the hazy, late afternoon, winter sun was about to disappear for the day.

They sat on the dashboard and looked at each other sadly. They moped for a while until Bear suddenly jumped so high, he bumped his head on the rear-view mirror.

"Wow, look at that!" he cried out.

They noticed that by stretching a bit they could see the rink and the bonfire.

It was beautiful. All kinds of people, big and small, were gliding around, as if guided by invisible magnets under the ice. Jingle Bells was playing through powerful loudspeakers. At the rim of the rink, there were some pine trees and a few benches. A dog was sitting next to the leftmost bench.

They seemed to recognize Hanna. She was skating with her red backpack, gliding around merrily, laughing and falling and getting up and then skating again. She was always next to Phil. He seemed to be teasing or chasing her. They sometimes sat down on the wooden bench, close to the bonfire. The dog went up to them and sat down. Bear had a new ambition: one day both he and Nosey would be inside that backpack skating with Hanna. She looked OK.

The animals were enchanted by the music and the beautiful winter scene. After watching the rink for quite a while, they went back to the duffle bag.

"This wasn't what we had expected Nosey, but it was still beautiful." And with these words, Bear and Nosey dug their heads into the remaining contents of the duffle bag, and they both fell fast asleep, dreaming about a time when they would all skate together.

One day...

Chapter Five

Midnight Adventure
Part 1

It was a long ride and Bear and Nosey were jolted awake when the car went over a big bump. Bear sat upright and looked for his friend who was waving his left ear slowly back and forth while producing an enormous, sleepy yawn. The animals could only see each other's silhouettes because it was quite dark. The crescent moon was just a little fatter this time than the night before. It took Bear a little while to realize just exactly where they were.

"Nosey, I think we are going home from skating," he whispered.

"Where else would they go at this hour?" he added.

"To the Midnight Madness then, right? I have the red bag with the clock we need to return," they heard Hanna say.

"Yep," Phil responded.

Bear straightened up and knocked his head really hard against a gift box.

"Lucky I'm a rag bear or I'd have a bump the size of a coconut growing on my head," he muttered.

"Did you hear that?" he whispered. "Something fantastic may happen today still! Let's move over to the red bag quietly, and be prepared to look like real plush animals. There are some price-tags here we can put on ourselves. We'll just behave like toys if someone sees us. Ah, this is great. If we have a bit of luck, we can join these guys and go to some place where they celebrate madness at midnight." Bear's eyes were gleaming with joy.

"What do you think Midnight Madness is, Nosey?" he asked his friend eagerly and Nosey's imagination was going wild.

"Midnight Madness was first celebrated a long, long time ago when there was a full moon two days before Christmas. People lit candles and went out at midnight to sing Christmas carols, and the celebrations turned into a big Midnight Madness. Soon it was celebrated in many cities, including Burlington."

Bear nodded, and then he had an idea.

"What do you think of this one?" he whispered all fired up.

"I think, Midnight Madness started in the forests. We all know that animals are more active when there is a full moon. People saw that the animals of the forest were having a great time one midnight before Christmas when there was a full moon. They were jumping around wildly, flapping their tails and ears and eating a lot. So, the people decided to copy the animals and called it Midnight Madness."

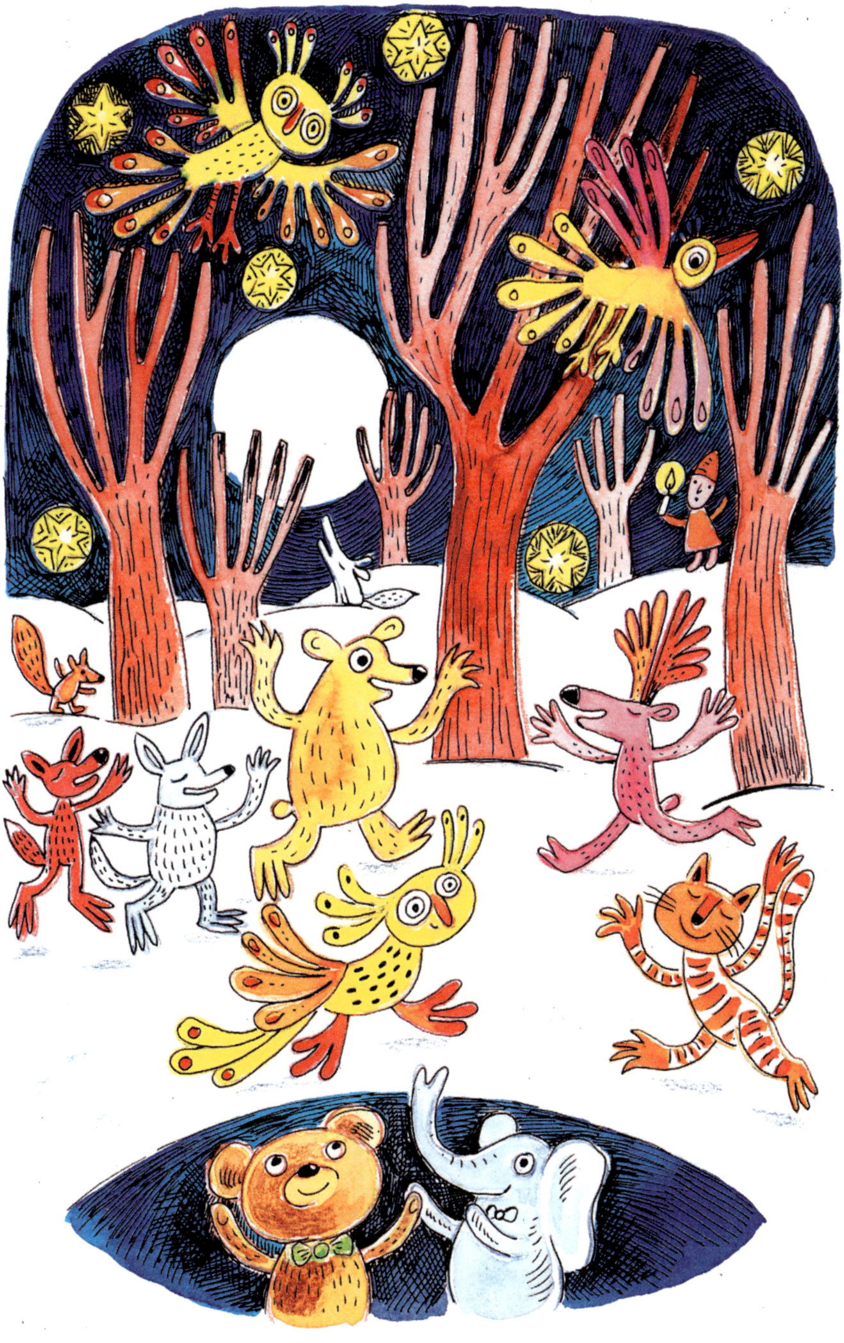

The car turned into a parking lot and stopped. There was some commotion again.

"We've got the bungee cords here, right?" Hanna asked.

"Yep. We're all ready to pick up the most beautiful Christmas tree in the world," Phil said.

Bear loved Christmas trees. They were so mystical and mighty and filled with surprises

"This is great. Nosey, there will be a Christmas tree in the house for sure."

They heard the car doors slam, and the animals were left in the car again.

"It's OK Nosey. I understand this one. They'll buy the tree and then we'll go to the Midnight Madness. Let's get

on the dashboard and watch them buy their Christmas tree. But remember, when we see them come back towards the car, we'll have to get back here real fast."

The animals climbed out of the red bag, and with a few jumps they were on the dashboard. They could see a big sign that said:

CHRISTMAS TREES

"Look, there they are," Bear said, and he pushed his muzzle against the windshield, flattening it completely.

Three flood lights lit the small place where the trees were sold. There was a truck, a few dozen Christmas trees and Joe, the merry Christmas tree vendor. He drove down to Ontario all the way from Prince Edward Island each year, with a truckload of trees to sell before Christmas. His plan was to sell all of his trees, and then return to his family with a truckload of Christmas presents. His family liked that, and so did Joe. He rubbed his big red palms together and turned towards his new customers.

"Anything in particular you're looking for? I still have some Scotch pines right over here and a few firs in the corner there."

"It should be plump and bushy and taper off nicely towards the top," Phil said.

"Could we see the firs?" Hanna asked and they both moved to the far corner.

Some trees were suspended from their tips, others were lying around on their sides.

"This is a bit small," he said.

"It should go all the way up to the ceiling, don't you think?" she asked.

"Of course, it should. Look at this one. This one looks really nice," Phil said.

"Yeah, it's the nicest one," the couple said almost at the same time, so that settled the fate of an exceptionally bushy fir.

Snow started falling as the tree was readied for the journey to its new home, making the evening even more magical.

Joe appeared, put on his gloves and offered to carry the tree to the car.

In the meantime, the animals found themselves in trouble. Nosey's right foot got stuck in the cup holder.

"Come on, Nosey, I'll pull. We've just got to get into the red bag before they get into the car," pleaded Bear.

Nosey tried to pull his foot out but couldn't. His friend pulled at him as hard as he could, but the foot would not budge. Bear was in his element.

"Hang in there, Nose!"

Nosey could only see traces of Bear here and there, he was jumping around with such speed. In less than a minute, he created a giant sling by stretching out a bungee cord between the two front door window cranks. He weighed down the section above the passenger seat with a bag he filled with pop cans. The bungee cord lowered until it was just within Nosey's reach.

"OK Nose, grab the cord and hang on tight," he told his

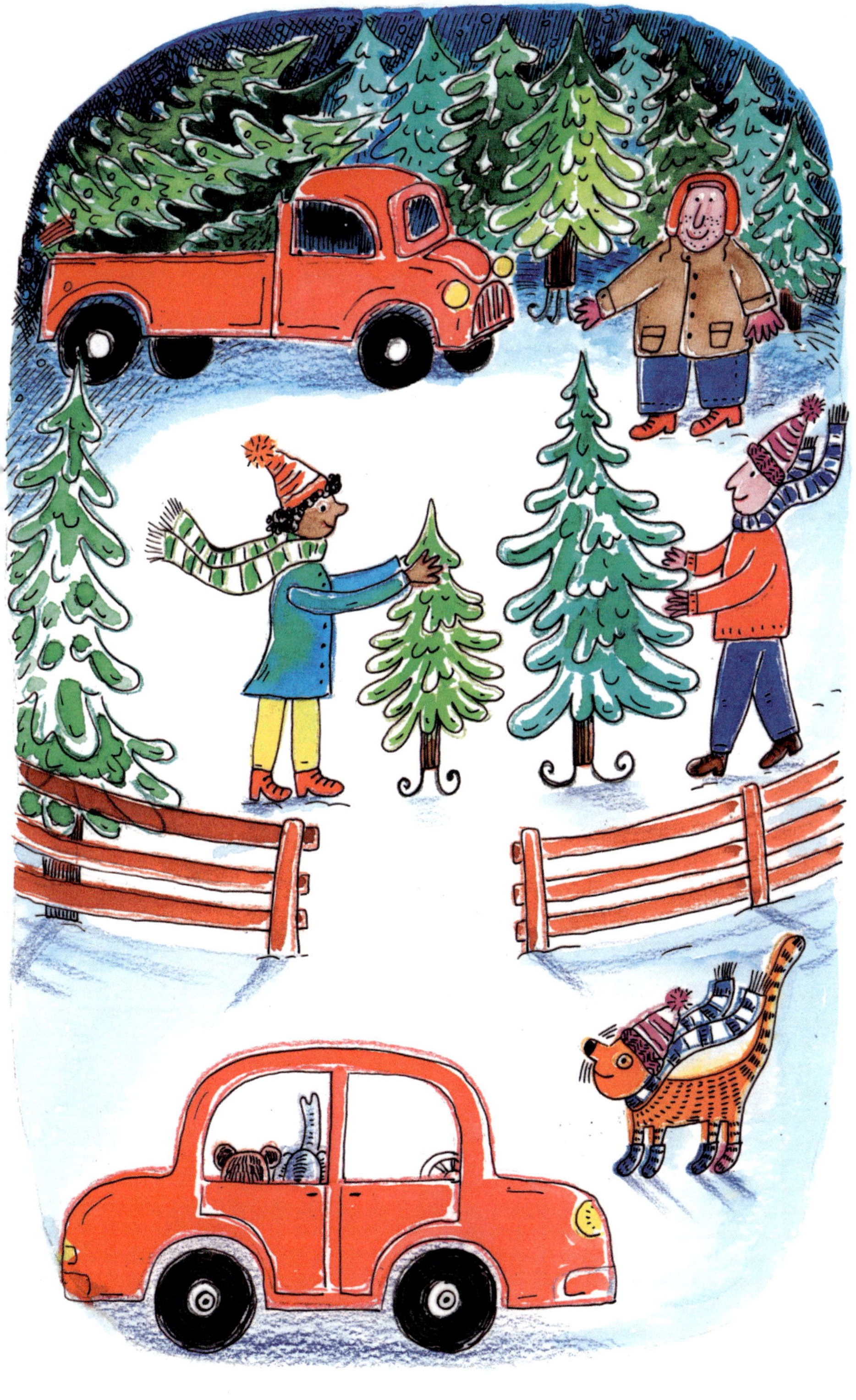

friend. Once Bear was sure that Nosey had a firm grip on the cord, he poured out the contents of the bag and Nosey was ejected from the cup holder, right onto the back seat. Phew!

"WOW!!! That was great," rejoiced Bear, but he hardly had time to unhook the bungee cord from the driver's side when they heard the familiar metallic sound of keys rattling in the lock.

The animals disappeared into the red bag. They covered themselves at the last second, and they heard the couple looking for the bungee cord because they wanted to secure the Christmas tree on the roof rack with it.

"I remember seeing it on the back seat..." Hanna said.

"Well, it's not here," Phil responded.

"Hey, how did it get here?" she asked, pulling it out from the foot of the passenger seat.

"Well, we really need it, so it's a good thing you found it," he said.

"That was close, Nosey, ... but this is really going to be fun! You'll see," Bear whispered. He had no idea what exactly would happen, because they still didn't know what Midnight Madness was. He was absolutely positive, though, that it would be something they had never experienced before.

Part 2

Soon the engine revved up and the two animals were finally on their way to Midnight Madness, whatever that was. The car stopped and the back door was opened.

"Holy Polar Bear," Bear would have liked to scream, because they were actually being lifted up.

The animals were deep inside the red bag and, therefore, they couldn't see a thing. In a few minutes however, they could hear Christmas carols, the shuffling of busy feet, laughter and excited whispers.

Bear decided to try to pierce two tiny peeping-holes in the bag: one for his friend and one for himself. He was tremendously curious. He found a pin and worked on piercing the holes. Just as he was done, the speakers boomed up:

> "You better watch out
> You better not cry
> You better not pout
> I'm telling you why
> .... Santa Claus is coming to town."

Bear got really nervous when he heard "He sees when you are bad or good so be good..." so he just had to explain this to Santa.

"Sorry Santa, but I had to do this, and I didn't really ruin the bag..." he bargained, as he pressed his right eye to the hole he had pierced and told his friend to do the same.

What they saw was unlike anything they had ever seen in their whole lives.

Everything was practically swimming in Christmas lights and decorations. People with happy faces were carrying fully loaded shopping bags, thinking of the excitement and joy they would bring to their loved ones and wondering what kind of surprises might be awaiting them.

Toys seemed to be everywhere - on display in front of shops, inside shops and sticking out of the shopping bags that people were carrying around. Just after they passed a model train display table, they saw Santa's mailbox.

"Look, Nosey! This is how it all works. That's the post office where people drop off their letters addressed to Santa." The sign read:

Santa Claus
North Pole
H0H 0H0
Canada

"See? Elves open the mail and sort the letters. I guess one pile is from bad kids and the other is from good kids. Then, the elves deliver the two piles of mail to Santa. And then Santa mixes the mail up, because he's a good guy and he doesn't punish anyone, so everyone gets a present."

They were carried in and out of stores. They saw tons of exciting toys and gadgets of all sorts. In one store, different colourful spinning objects were displayed in the dark and illuminated by black light, which made them sparkle brightly and magically. The animals were enchanted. And the most special part of the night was just about to begin! They saw big arrows that read:

"Santa's Village."

Nosey whispered, "Are we really going to see Santa?" and Bear nodded. This was beginning to be a very serious matter.

There were lots of people and stores here. The animals saw blow-pens, spinning tops that lit up and doodled and funny boomerangs. They soon saw the actual sign that read "Santa's Village." What the animals spotted took their breath away. Santa himself was sitting in a gigantic green armchair in front of his hut, carefully listening to

children's wishes. His beard was white and curly and his jolly white moustache curled up and covered part of his rosy, red cheeks. There were elves helping him and a very long line of children and parents waited eagerly to talk to him. Bear looked around and came up with a brave idea.

Part 3

Santa's Village was on the main floor in the mall, in an atrium setting. There was an escalator leading to the second floor where a high wire from one end of the second-floor railing stretched to the other. It ran right above Santa's armchair. Reindeer and a balancing elf were going across the wire from one end to the other.

"Wait here Nose, be right back," he told his friend, and he managed to get out of the bag while Hanna was looking at some gifts. He dashed towards the escalator, and was up at the railing in an instant. The view from above was so breathtaking that he stopped for a second, but he knew he had to act fast. Keeping one eye on Nosey below and another on the approaching elf, he decided to borrow the elf's balancing rod and slide above Santa's head.

"Sorry elf," he said, as he put him on the ledge and held the balancing device in his own paws.

As if Bear had been practicing sliding up and down on high wires all his life, he slid right above Santa's head.

"This better work," he whispered, and he jumped straight into Santa's lap, just as a child was leaving.

Santa was certainly used to miracles but even he was very surprised to find a bear land in his lap from out of the blue.

He slid his right hand over his white beard, and held Bear gently in his left.

"Well, hello Bear! I'm sure you have a special wish for Christmas, am I right?" he inquired kindly.

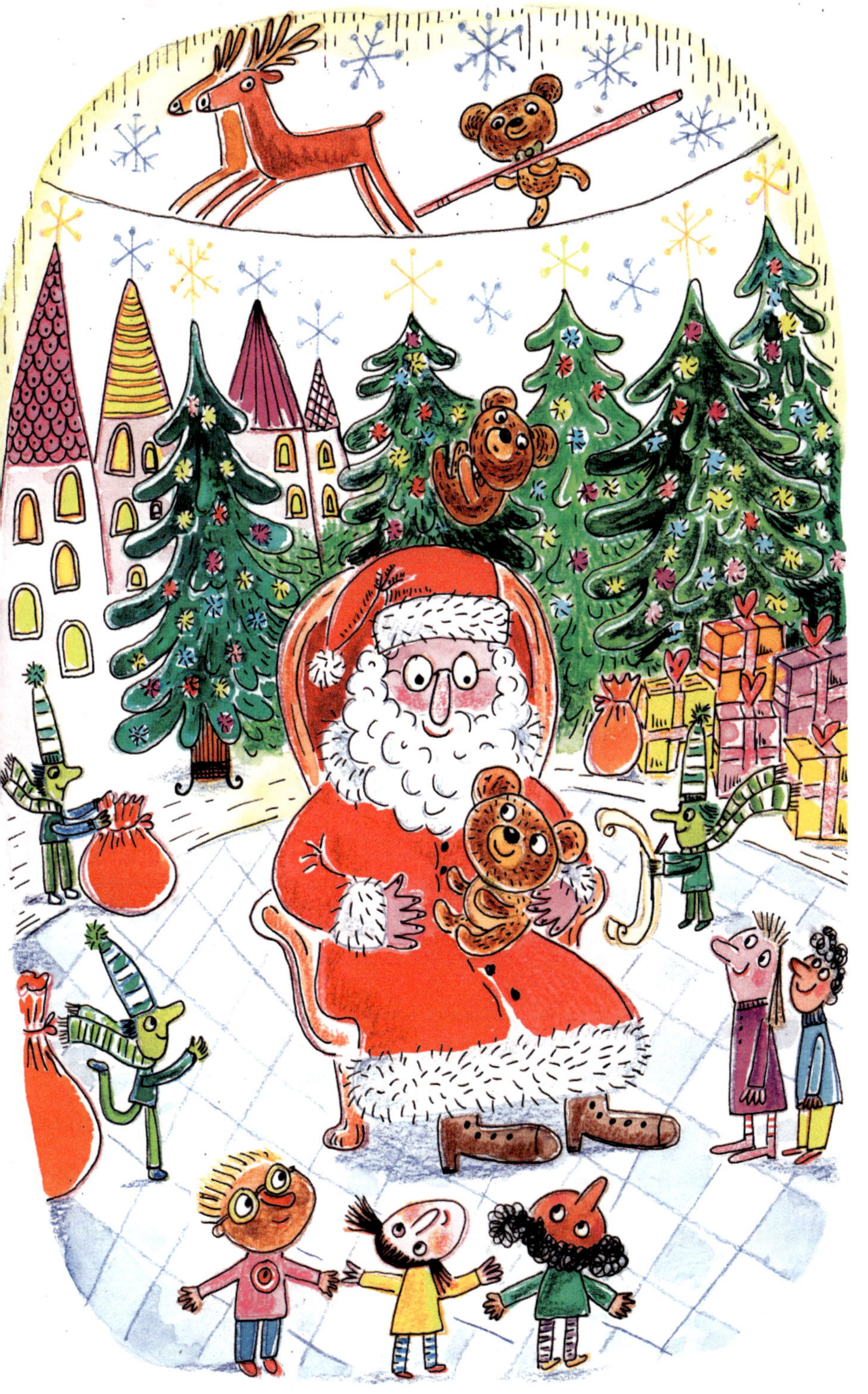

Bear struggled to find the words that he had been preparing to say; he was so overcome by the magical joy that now filled him.

After a hesitant clearing of his throat, all the words suddenly came rushing out.

"Hi, Santa. Thank you for asking about my special wish. I do have one. You see, it's kind of an emergency. I know I wasn't always good, especially when we ran away from the toy store and got into all kinds of mischief to get here, but my best friend, Nosey and I, have a wish we would like more than anything for Christmas." He paused and searched the kind eyes that peered at him through a pair of wire-framed glasses.

"Dear Santa," Bear continued, "We'd really like a family. Actually, the very one where we are hiding now. You know them, don't you? They seem to be really nice people, and I think we would be very happy together."

Bear stopped here, trying to find some kind of a sign that would reveal whether he was asking too much or not, but there was no telling. Santa listened patiently, as kind and generous as ever. He finally held Bear a bit closer to him and said, "Well, I have been keeping an eye on you Bear. You are a bit naughty but certainly goodhearted, aren't you?"

On hearing this, Bear wanted to turn back time and undo all the naughty things he had ever done, but since that was impossible, he just waited in tense excitement for Santa to go on.

"You seem to be taking good care of your friend, Nosey. That's good."

Bear sighed a tiny breath of relief and nodded.

"So," and Santa waved to one of the elves who scribbled down Bear's wish, "Thank you for coming by, and we'll see what we can do about this special wish." He lowered Bear from his lap and as he released him, he added, "Have a very Merry Christmas!"

Stunned, Bear just sat there, his head spinning. His wish was on the list! He had to tell this to Nosey right away. He looked at Santa gratefully and said in a very thin voice, "Thank you, Santa. Merry Christmas!"

He knew he had no more time to spare, so he dashed off in the direction where he saw a glimpse of the red shopping bag. To his horror it was moving and then it disappeared from his sight.

He ran as fast as he could, but instead of one, he saw a million shopping bags, and none were red.

"Now what am I going to do?" Bear said in despair.

He decided not to do anything for a few moments, because he was afraid, he might do something silly. He thought hard. Going back to the car was not an option, because he had no idea where the car was parked. Making an announcement through the PA system: "Lady with red shopping bag please meet Bear at the information desk," made him think of at least twenty ladies lining up. Bear knew that a lot of adult ladies seemed to be crazy about teddy bears, and irresistible as he was, they may start fighting over him and he may end up with the wrong lady. So, this didn't sound like a good idea either.

As he was thinking hard, he spotted a red bag in the distance. He dashed towards it, but it was the wrong person with the wrong bag. Bear was getting exhausted and he wanted to cry. Not only was he going to miss his chance of having a family, but he had also lost his best friend in the process. And although a bear never gives up, he really didn't know what to do this time. He finally collapsed and looked behind him aimlessly. Right there he saw a pair of familiar ears flapping slowly back and forth.

"Nosey?" Bear screamed. "I got so scared!" and he rushed towards Nosey, who, to his dismay, was not in the red bag either.

"Nosey, where's the bag?"

His friend calmly pointed with his trunk at Hanna who was standing in a very slow-moving line right next to them.

"I was so scared I had lost you," and saying this, he hugged his friend and they jumped into the bag together.

"I might have a really great surprise for you," said Bear.

They could feel that they were lifted up, and carried out of the mall. They heard car keys and two car doors slam and the car engine start up. Both animals were so exhausted that they collapsed at the bottom of the red bag, covered by Christmas presents.

Outside, the snow was drifting gently and the car was heading home to Maple Avenue. With the Christmas tree on the roof rack, the car went through many side roads that were twinkling with Christmas lights and passed houses with smoke puffing from chimneys.

The four passengers, two of them sound asleep, were dreaming about a very special Christmas.

Chapter Six

Trip to Niagara Falls
Part 1

The winter sun peeked into the treasure chest room where Bear and Nosey were sitting at the bottom of the red bag. They were silent and motionless, their eyes wide open. They thought of all the things that had happened to them since they'd arrived in Burlington. As if they were watching a movie, they saw Burlington lit up with Christmas lights when they were landing, the long walk to Maple Avenue in the dark, the meowing incident, the elevator they created, Bear's detective mission the next day and Nosey's adventures the following night. When they finally thought about the skating, the Midnight Madness when people did their last-minute shopping till midnight, Santa, and how Bear almost got lost, they realized that they were still sitting inside the red shopping bag. This ended their daydream, and they jumped up with a start, sending a shower of small gifts flying around the room in all directions.

"Nosey!" exclaimed Bear.

"I talked to Santa yesterday," and he happily realized it hadn't been a dream after all.

"Something great is going to happen soon. I can feel it in my stuffing."

"These guys are cool. They brought us right back." He said looking around, not understanding why they had been so generously carried back to their hiding spot. He had important things to figure out now. Was it a good idea that he had asked Santa for this very family without discussing it with Nosey?

He started pacing back and forth in the little room, thinking out loud. He picked up the toys that were in his way, tossed them towards the chest while Nosey was busily constructing a new creation.

"Wow, Nosey, that's a beautiful seesaw! It'll be much more fun to get in and out of the chest now," praised Bear, with appreciation. This made Nosey very happy.

Bear didn't even know it yet, but his friend had done more than just one useful thing while Bear was talking: he had lifted fingerprints off some of the toys and compared them with the ones Bear got off the kitchen pot. He pointed meaningfully towards the fingerprint kit with his nose.

"Nosey, when on earth did

you do this?" he asked surprised, while examining and comparing the prints.

Nosey sat there smiling, feeling deeply proud of himself. He knew they were getting closer and closer to solving the mystery.

"OK, Nose. Let's see. This is a big discovery. The fingerprints you got off the toys match the prints I lifted off the pot. There are actually two types of prints you got from the toys, but they are nearly the same size. Because of this, we now know that..." and without finishing his sentence, he jumped high into the air.

"You know what this means, Nosey? It's just the four of us in this house. Come, let's talk this over," he said, and he sat down on one side of the seesaw.

Nosey sat down on the other side, and as they went up and down, Bear tried to sort out everything by asking questions of his friend, who either nodded or shook his head.

"OK, Nosey, do you like Phil?"

Nosey nodded.

"He looks OK to me too. Do you think we can trust him?"

Nosey nodded once again.

"I guess we can take the risk. Now, do like Hanna?" asked Bear.

Nosey nodded again.

"Do you think we can trust her?" Bear asked.

Nosey nodded happily, again.

"Do you like spaghetti with chocolate?" asked Bear

suddenly. This made Nosey shake his head so fast, he almost fell off the seesaw. He had no idea what spaghetti was, and for some reason he imagined it was a twelve-eyed monster that grabs elephants at night.

"It's OK Nosey, I'm sorry, I didn't mean to scare you. I was just checking if you were paying attention. Let's continue." Bear thought of the next question.

"Do you think we should stay here?" he asked.

Nosey nodded his head again.

"We're going to need some kind of a miracle and you know who takes care of miracles on Christmas Eve, don't you, Nosey?"

For a while, the animals just continued seesawing in silence, thinking about Santa Claus.

Their quiet game was interrupted by noises coming from the neighbouring room. They jumped off the seesaw and ran for cover.

"When did these guys come upstairs?"

"Nosey, I have an idea. Do you remember what's behind this treasure chest? The wardrobe, right?"

"Well, if we create an escape route to the wardrobe, we'll gain another hiding place, but we would also be

91

closer to their room and we might be able to hear what they are planning."

"Let's do it." he invited his friend.

Nosey disappeared then reappeared, dragging something.

"What on earth is that?" asked Bear.

Nosey was very proud that he could teach his friend how a stethoscope worked. He carefully put two ends of the object into Bear's ears, and then pressed the third flat end to the wall.

"Wow!" whispered Bear. "I can hear them talking. I can hear every word."

"It's almost time to go," said Phil. "Christmas shopping at Niagara Falls will be fun!"

"OK. I'll get the boxes of toys we are dropping off for

the Christmas toy drive and Jimmy's gift from the hobby room," Hanna said.

"We'll drop them all off at the Waterdown Plaza and we will be at Niagara Falls by four o'clock."

The moment Bear heard this he dragged the surprised Nosey by his tail to the gift-bags that were lined up near the window.

"Quick, Nosey, we have no time to lose. We have to look for the scissors and for a gift tag that says Jim or Jimmy. We also need the price tags, just in case."

Bear had everything organized in a matter of seconds, so they were soon crouching inside Jimmy's gift-bag. Just in time, because the door flung open and they could feel they were being lifted up.

"Here we go again..." whispered Bear, grabbing on tight to his friend.

They were carried down the stairs, down the hallway, and then, they heard the door slam shut. After a few seconds they were put down outside and heard the footsteps fade away.

"I'll carve some peeping holes. Don't worry, Nosey, they'll soon take us to the car."

They waited and waited, but no one seemed to come and pick them up.

"This is fishy. I guess we should start walking," Bear said and looked for his scissors.

"Good thing I brought these. I'll cut an opening at the bottom of this bag and we can simply walk to the car. It's not that far away." Saying this, Bear was already cutting away while Nosey grew more and more worried.

"There. Ready to go." and he started walking towards the car.

Just as they took a couple of steps, they heard voices and were hoisted up before they could say "Jiminy Cricket."

"Oh, my!" they gasped. Bear almost fell through the opening, which as it turned out, was almost too big. Nosey leapt to his rescue, grabbing him with his trunk at the last second.

"We made it. That was a close call, again..."

They were soon placed on the back seat and the car started moving.

"Nosey, do you agree that we should stay with these guys rather than being given to Jimmy?"

Nosey agreed so they got out of the gift bag quietly and hid under some blankets.

The sun was on its way down, but it was a bright, late afternoon. There was snow here and there on the ground, although most of it had melted during the day. The car stopped for a few minutes at the Waterdown Plaza before they got going again.

"It might be snowing at Niagara Falls!" thought Bear, and he secretly hoped it was.

Part 2

"Nosey, I think it's safe to peek out. We must be on the highway. This car is fast."

"Let's play," invited Nosey, pointing to a Niagara Falls coupon booklet with his trunk.

"OK, ten questions about Niagara Falls," said Bear.

Nosey was excited because he had picked up some bits and pieces of information about Niagara Falls from a picture book the previous day and he was hoping to surprise his friend.

The game reminded Bear of Grandma Brun, a very old lady bear at the toy store who taught him a lot of interesting facts, as well as wise and naughty things, and she took care of him when he was little. Her name was Brunhilda, but Bear just called her Brunma or Grandma Brun. She was OK with this so Bear figured that she was, in fact, his grandmother.

The animals took turns asking each other questions.

"Ok, Nosey, what is the origin of the word Niagara?"

"Onguiaahra," Nosey said in a split second, very proudly swinging his ears.

It was his turn to ask the next question.

"What does Onguiaahra mean?"

"Rolling waters," responded Bear.

"Incorrect! It means the strait," beamed Nosey.

"Ah yes, it's a First Nation Iroquoian word, got it," said Bear.

"Do the fish that go over Niagara Falls fly, die or survive, Nosey?"

"Die for sure," grimaced his friend.

"90%, which means nine out of ten fish, survive! That's a fact," corrected Bear and forgetting to take turns, he just went on and on asking questions. Poor Nosey's head felt like it was getting bigger and bigger, until he noticed that his friend had begun reading out of a booklet about the Falls once he'd run out of information of his own. With this, Nosey jumped up and kindly pummeled Bear with the booklet because by now he already knew everything and more that any self-respecting elephant ever needs to know about Niagara Falls.

"Duck, Nosey," whispered Bear. I saw a sign that said, "Falls - follow 420 or something. We'll probably be there in a few minutes."

The car slowed down, turned right at the traffic lights and soon they were driving up Clifton Hill. They saw millions of lights and colourful Christmas displays.

"Look at that! We've got to get a closer look. We must!"

"These guys will probably decide when they'll meet back at the car. If we can find out, getting back will be easy. All we have to do is arrive a bit before them, hide under the car and jump in while they are loading up." Bear paused.

"Getting out is trickier, though…"

"I've got it!" he exclaimed, as he spotted a balloon on the back seat.

"Nosey, can you quickly blow up this balloon?"

In just a minute, Nosey blew up a big, fat balloon.

"We can only park here for an hour, but that should be enough," the animals heard Phil say.

"OK. Let's meet here at five and then drive down to the Falls to see the Christmas lights on the way home," Hanna replied.

"This is great," muttered Bear, and as the couple was getting out, Bear released the air from the balloon. The whistling noise made Phil open the back door of the car to look around. This gave the animals just enough time to jump onto the ledge and with another jump they disappeared under the car.

"I don't understand..." they heard Phil say, and of course he couldn't see anything because the balloon had already shrunk back to its original size and was lying once again innocently on the car seat.

"Well, let's get going," said Phil.

The couple disappeared in opposite directions hoping to find some great last-minute stocking stuffers for each other. The animals could hardly believe this moment had arrived.

They had plans. From under the car they could see a million feet, but they were not afraid.

They had learned from their toy store days, how to jump between legs without being stepped on.

Their plan was to get a good view of Clifton Hill by getting onto a shelf where other plush animals were displayed.

"OK, Nosey. You know the old trick still, I hope. Blend in and if anyone reaches in your direction, you push the closest stuffy in front of you and hide behind it. It has always worked, so far.

Nosey reminded his friend that they could also do the "defective look" trick. He always enjoyed doing that.

If he pulled his trunk in, he looked like a pig with the body and ears of an elephant. No one had ever found that appealing. As for Bear, well, irresistible as he was, he could actually distort himself so much that he was known to have made little children cry.

"OK, Nosey, we know the rules. We keep close together and the car never leaves our sight. Ready? Let's go!"

And so, the animals hopped along merrily in the bustling crowd, while Bear read the signs out loud to Nosey, who was just learning how to read.

"Ripley's Believe It or Not Museum,
The Haunted House,
Circus World,
Guinness World of Records,
Fun House,
The Adventure Dome,
The House of Frankenstein,"

"Wow, Nose, this is incredible! We've got to come back here one day to check out all these things. One hour is hardly enough. Look there!" and Bear pointed to an arcade game centre that also had several bean-toss stations.

"Let's go there. That'll be fun!"

Soon the animals were watching a sea of people ready to take their best shots to win a stuffy.

One kid aimed a little too high, so Bear leaned forward from behind an angry tiger to check if Nosey was OK. Right then another kid who had won a prize started screaming.

"I want that bear up there. The one with the green tie." A hand was already reaching towards Bear.

Nosey leapt to his friend's rescue and knocked all the other angry tigers off the shelf, together with a bunch of bumblebees and beavers. While the attendant was cleaning up the mess, Bear and Nosey were able to escape, comfortably.

"Wow, thanks Nosey! You saved me, again." Bear hugged his friend.

"I guess that was enough of an adventure for today. Let's go back to the car. It's almost five."

Bear and Nosey were hopping back towards the car, carefully avoiding being stepped on, when Bear's attention was suddenly drawn to a weeping fire hydrant.

"Nosey, pinch me please. It's only possible that this fire hydrant is crying if we are in a story book." Nosey shook his head and carried out Bear's wish obediently.

"Ouch!" cried out Bear, and he jumped right next to the fire hydrant, where he spotted a little girl who was sobbing bitterly. She was about five. Bear's heart twisted with pain and he wished that it was the fire hydrant producing the heartbroken sound, even at the expense of him having to turn into a cartoon character in a picture book.

"My, my," said Bear softly, as he hopped a bit closer to the little girl, not really knowing what to do.

She looked down at him with red eyes and after a few sniffs, she asked, "Are you lost too?"

Bear shook his head, which made the little girl cry again.

"Now, why is it so bad that I'm not lost?" wondered Bear, but he also realized he had to help somehow.

"What's your name?" he asked her.

"Melanie Hopkins," she responded and stopped crying.

"Look, Melanie. My friend Nosey and I will help you." Bear had no idea exactly how they'd do that, but he was sure he would not rest until he came up with an idea.

Melanie picked up Bear and hugged him. Then she whispered into his ears.

"Will you find my mom for me? I wandered away to look at the toys while she was trying on some gloves. Mom is the kindest and prettiest lady in the world, so you shouldn't have a problem finding her." A faint smile came to her face as she looked at Bear, hopefully.

"Don't be afraid Melanie. We'll find your mom." His thoughts were racing because he had a difficult task to solve. He rubbed his furry head against Melanie's face, which surprised him because he wasn't used to being kind to little girls. In his toy store days, he would hide from them, and he often made fun of them, although he knew that it wasn't a nice thing to do. Now he found himself helping and caring for this little girl.

"Nosey, we have to help Melanie. We might not get back to the car by five." His friend was in full agreement. The thought that their good deed may cost them their ride home and they may lose their chance at belonging to a family made Bear dizzy, but this was no time to feel sorry for themselves. Melanie was in trouble, and he knew that if he was fast and tricky enough, they could help her.

It was seven minutes to five!

Part 3

Bear came up with a plan. They would have to get Melanie to the car. Bear was absolutely sure that if the couple saw Melanie crying, they would call the police and Melanie could then find her mom.

In the meantime, Melanie noticed Nosey, so she crouched down and picked him up too. Bear grabbed this opportunity and said, "OK, Melanie, hang on to Nosey and follow me. We're going to get help." Melanie nodded.

Bear was hopping along as fast as he could. They were very close to the car, but they only had minutes left. As soon as Bear spotted the car, he noticed with dismay that the lights were already on and it was pulling out of the parking spot.

"Oh no!" he cried out, "We've got to stop them." and as luck would have it, traffic was moving so slowly that Bear had enough time to come up with another idea. The car was very close to a pedestrian crossing. If Bear could press the button, the lights would turn red, the cars would have to stop and they would have enough time to put their plan into action.

Bear ran to the crossing and started jumping in mid-air, to push the button. He finally succeeded, and the lights turned green for pedestrians and red for the cars.

"OK, guys come with me," he said and waived to Melanie and Nosey. "We have to get close enough to the car so that Hanna and Phil can spot Melanie."

Turning to Melanie, he said, "Look, Melanie, you will

have to say goodbye to Nosey now because the couple in that green car will help you. You should stay on the sidewalk, and when they notice you, please wave to them and cry a bit, if possible. But only for a short time, because

105

once they get out of the car, you'll be OK. Bye, Melanie! Good luck and Merry Christmas!" and with this, Bear hopped up to Melanie and gently flapped his right ear on her cheeks, but there was no time for hugs and goodbyes. Turning to Nosey, he said, "Nosey, please say goodbye to Melanie, we've got to run now," and sure enough, he was already just a foot away from the car.

When Nosey flapped a big kiss on Melanie's cheeks and jumped down, she started crying bitterly, again.

Bear was already jumping up and down frantically next to the passenger window, producing a knock with his plastic nose at each jump.

The window was rolled down finally, and Bear almost landed inside the car. His special jumping skills saved him.

"Phil, I thought I was seeing things, but something small and furry actually appeared at my window... Hey, look. There's a little girl, all alone, crying on the curb. I have to get out, she could be lost." And just as Hanna opened the door, the railway lights turned red a block further up Clifton Hill, so the whole line of cars were destined to stay just where they were for at least another six or seven minutes.

"Why are you crying?" Hanna asked kindly, as she approached the little girl.

"Is your mom around somewhere?"

Hanna could hardly understand what Melanie was saying, she was sobbing so hard.

"I lost my mom and Bear and Nosey. Please help me find them," she pleaded.

She picked up the little, sobbing girl, comforted her, and said, "It's alright. You're going to be fine. I can see an officer just around the corner there. She will help us."

They went up to her and explained that Melanie was lost. The officer disappeared inside a store and soon enough all the loudspeakers stopped playing Christmas carols. Instead, they heard a confident voice.

"Could Mrs. Hopkins come to the Circus World entrance, please? We have found Melanie. Mrs. Hopkins, please come to the Circus World entrance."

In a matter of minutes, a sobbing, beautiful, young lady appeared, running towards Melanie.

"Melanie!" she cried out, when she saw her daughter.

"Mommy, I thought I'd lost you! A bear and an elephant and this nice lady helped me."

The exhausted and very happy mom didn't understand a word about bears and elephants, she was just trying to find the right words to thank the two helpful people.

"I really don't know how I can ever thank you," she said, with tears in her eyes.

"Please accept this, and have a very Merry Christmas!" With these words she handed over a huge gift bag to Hanna and the police woman, despite their protests, she waved goodbye and soon disappeared with her daughter.

"Wow, that was a nice way to end this scare. Thanks, officer... Merry Christmas!"

Hanna shouted in the direction of the officer, as she sat back in the car with the gift bag, and rolled up her window.

"Merry Christmas!" she shouted back.

Phil watched the events, happy and proud of his wife.

"It's so wonderful you could help make a little girl's Christmas," he said, and the couple hugged each other.

The train finally passed, and the railway crossing was clear once again.

"What do you say we make a loop, and check out those Christmas lights before we go home?" he suggested, and turned on the radio, smiling.

You may be wondering where Bear and Nosey were at this point.

They had a bit of a problem sneaking back into the car through the passenger door, unnoticed, but thankfully, they had succeeded. All four were in the car again. Bear, Nosey, Phil and Hanna were together, heading towards the Christmas lights.

They soon came upon a dazzling, animated light display of Disney characters all twinkling in the dark. They saw Snow White and the seven dwarfs, Cinderella, and even Donald Duck with Huey, Dewey and Louie. A band was playing at the foot of the display, and as they slowly drove on, they soon approached Niagara Falls. The car stopped for a while near the Falls. The Falls looked mightier and more beautiful than ever. The incredible amount of water that rushed from its source, seemed to cascade down endlessly. It was remarkable.

It was a miraculous force. Wishes of centuries were swallowed up by its majestic, thundering flow.

Bear thought of Melanie, who would soon be comfy and cozy, drinking hot chocolate at home. Her Mom would

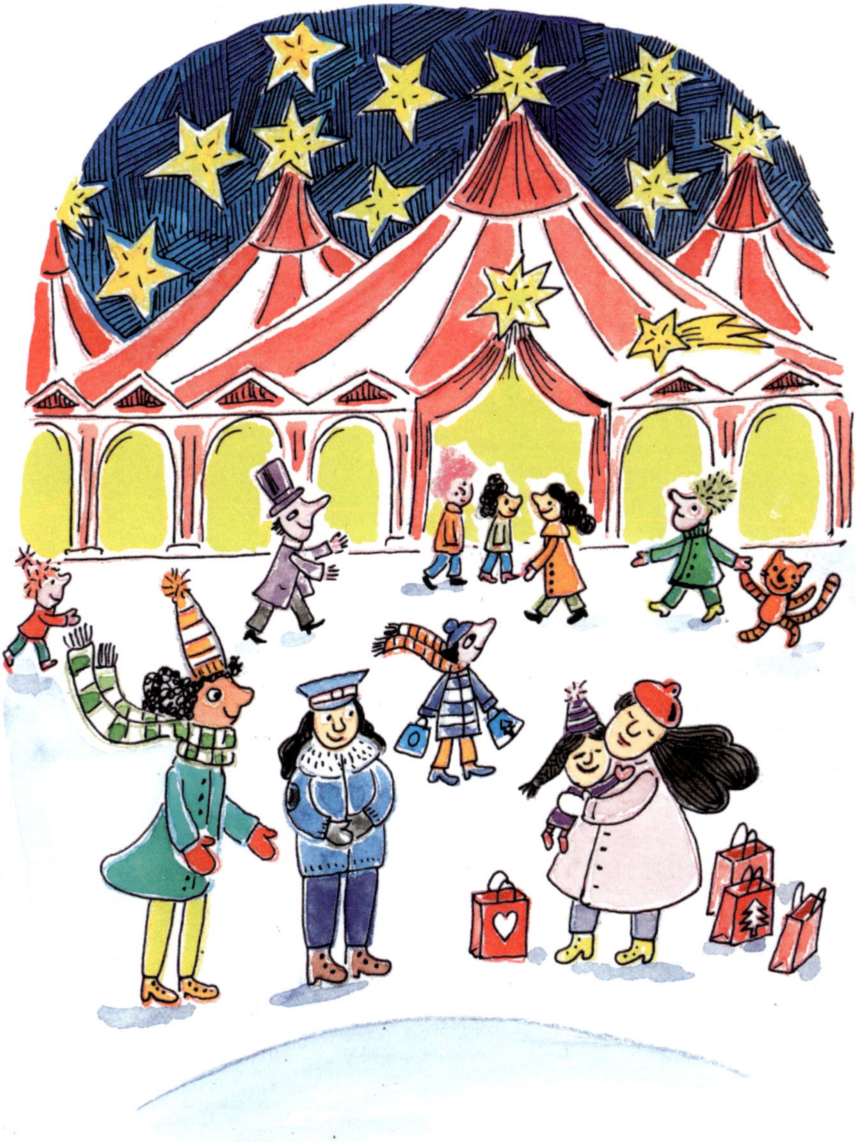

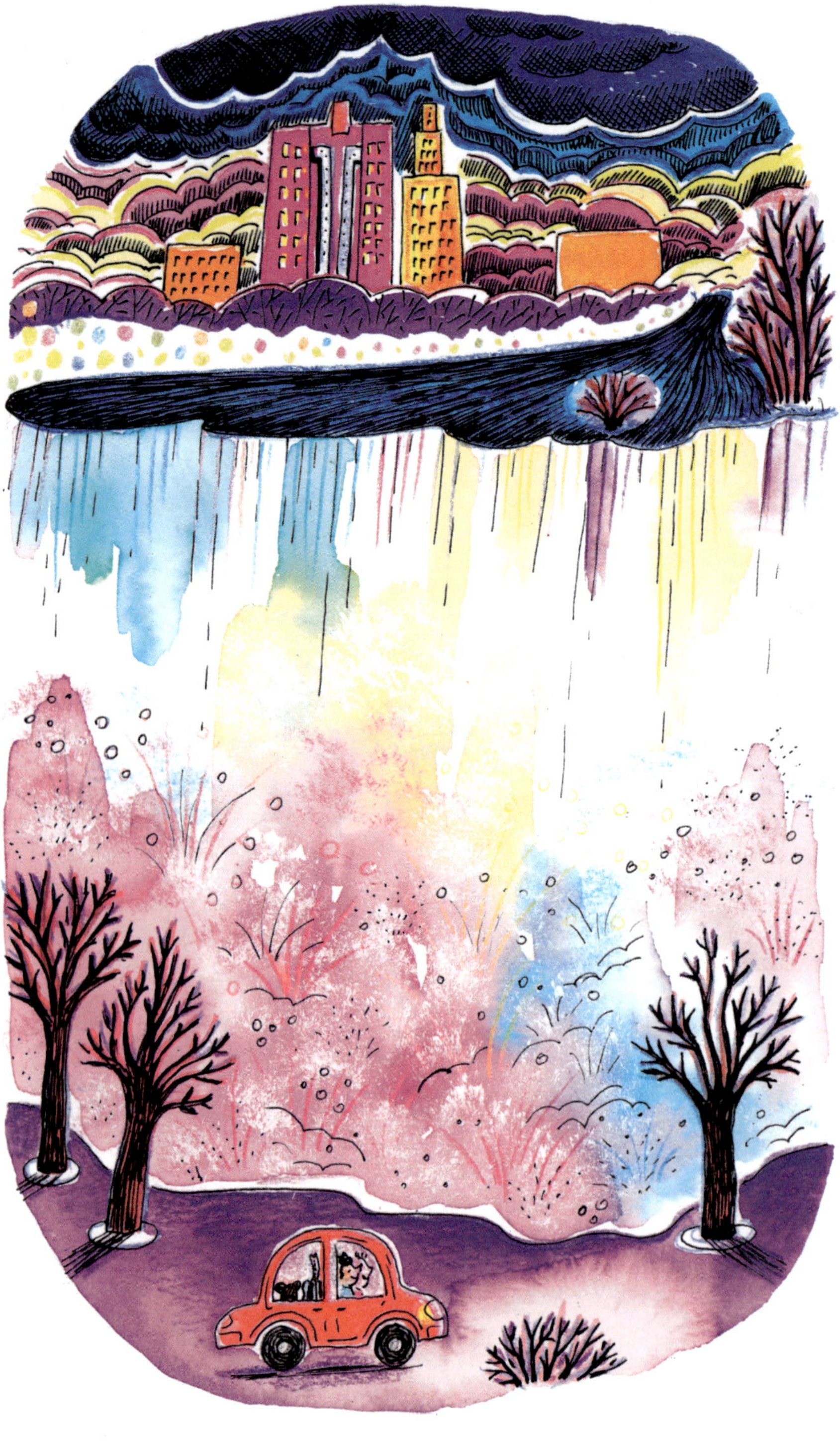

tuck her into bed and whisper in her ear, reminding her Christmas was just one more day away and Daddy would be home soon for Christmas, too.

Bear was very happy for the little girl and wished that they did not have to hide, but could jump around freely. He wished that Nosey could slurp hot chocolate too and that they would be tucked in at night, just like Melanie.

As the car pulled away slowly from the Falls, they were on their way home, and Bear felt the incredible force and power of the Falls. He once again thought of his meeting with Santa and knew he believed in Christmas miracles, more than ever.

Chapter Seven

**Here I am Bear!
Part 1**

Bear woke up earlier than usual. It was still dark outside. He poked around a bit, and found his way out of the bag. He saw the familiar treasure chest lit by the moonlight and sighed with a smile.

"Things seem to be working out quite well." He had plans.

"I need to make Nosey some Christmas presents before he wakes up," and with that thought he disappeared to the far corner of the room, near the window.

Nosey woke up too. This time, he was wide awake from the moment he opened his eyes. He had plans too, but just like Bear, he wanted to keep them a secret. Nosey heard his friend fumbling around in the dark, so he figured they were probably safe, back in the treasure chest room. He made holes at the bottom of the gift bag, just the way he had seen Bear do it the previous day and walked over to the treasure chest, in disguise. That's where he was collecting little bits and pieces of things from which he wanted to make his friend some beautiful Christmas presents.

Once he was at the chest, he sat on the seesaw, ready to go up.

"Uh-oh. This isn't moving. I need to find a way of getting up without Bear... Let's see... I think I would need..." he muttered to himself, and almost immediately spotted what he was looking for: a small bowling ball.

"This is quite heavy. It will work perfectly."

He hauled the ball to the side where he was sitting and rolled it over to the other side where Bear would normally sit. This did the trick, and Nosey was hoisted up to the edge of the chest.

He jumped in to look for the hidden treasures that he had prepared in advance: a small flashlight, some cardboard, a sheet of paper, scissors, glue, silver glitter, some shirts and a marker. He started working feverishly.

In the meanwhile, Bear was making a toy hot air balloon, and already had a balloon blown up. He was stretching out a hairnet that he wanted to pull over the balloon.

At first, his plump head got caught in the hairnet, but he then managed to release his head and pull the hairnet where it belonged: over the balloon. He attached a string to it so that it could be hung, and started making the gondola from a small paper cup.

"I'll hide my special gift inside the gondola," and he fished out something small all wrapped up.

Bear continued to make a sleigh from red cardboard.

"All done. All I have to do is make the Mikado pick-up sticks." He had taken forty-one toothpicks from the kitchen and kept this a secret. The toothpicks were ideal for the game. He had to put a yellow, a blue, a green or a red stripe on each, and the game was ready.

In the meantime, Nosey was carefully snipping nine red buttons off an old blouse, and he had an old blue shirt lined up for the same purpose. Once he had all eighteen pieces, he was ready to draw the Nine Men's Morris board. He had a piece of cardboard and a marker, so he put down his trunk carefully on the cardboard, traced the pen along it and drew a perfectly crooked line.

"Better straighten my trunk out," he thought, and flipped over the cardboard. He drew beautiful straight lines and soon he was ready with their favourite game.

Next, he made a Christmas card by drawing snowflakes on dark blue cardboard. He put glue over the drawing and covered it with silver glitter. After fanning off the excess sparkling dust with his ears, three beautiful snowflakes glistened on the cardboard, just like the ones he had drawn on the airplane window at the beginning of this whole adventure. Finally, he set out to fold a paper plane.

While the animals were working away, the sun came up and with it, some birds. There were several bird feeders in the backyard, so there was quite a party. It was the day of Christmas Eve, after all.

Nosey was all done and after hiding the gifts carefully, he made a kind of funny noise, trying to get his friend's attention.

"Come out, Nosey, let's play something. We can play till the first star comes up. Then, we'll have to sit on the windowsill, choose a Christmas tree for ourselves, and we can celebrate Christmas." There was a little sadness in his voice. He so wished they could spend Christmas with the couple, as a family. But then, he also knew that he had to be patient because miracles were never announced ahead of time. Right now, the best thing he could do was to plan a nice Christmas for his friend and himself.

The animals started to gather toys and lined them up in the order they would play with them. The hovercraft was first, the magnetic fishing game second. They played for hours and hours, and they were just about to get into a friendly discussion about whether they should play with the candle-making kit or the gyroscope next, when they heard noises coming from the stairs.

"Mighty Ursus Horribilis! How did they get here out of nowhere?" panicked Bear.

"Hide, Nosey, quick!"

However, there was no reason to panic. The footsteps were heard going down the stairs and were swallowed up in the thick padding of the dining room carpet.

Another set of footsteps, a bit heavier, followed in exactly the same manner.

"Nose, what do you think they are up to?" whispered Bear to his friend, almost disappointed that no one had come into the treasure chest room.

"Let's check it out, OK?" and Bear was already making a move, but Nosey wasn't all that sure that it was safe to venture out. Finally, his curiosity and love for adventure won out, as usual, so both animals started tiptoeing towards the door.

"You know, Nosey, they may have gone down to decorate the Christmas tree…"

"Or, Hanna is baking Christmas cookies and Phil is stealing the cookie dough when she's not looking. I'd like to try that once. I've heard it's delicious!"

"Or, if the cookies are ready, she may have told him that she would like to play hide-and-seek. Why you ask? Because while he is "it", she is hiding the cookies in the hatbox as fast as she can, so that Phil doesn't eat them all before Christmas," they laughed and giggled and giggled and laughed.

The animals went on and on guessing with great excitement what the couple might be doing, until they heard the doorbell ring.

"Hi, Tim!" they heard. And then after a while: "Thanks, we'll be right over."

"Nosey, it seems like they're leaving. If they do, we can sneak down. Let's listen."

"There's a Christmas party next door and they'd like us to drop by. Isn't that great? Our first Christmas party in Canada. Of course, they're all partying till midnight because almost everyone celebrates Christmas tomorrow morning on Christmas Day," they heard.

"Well, lucky for us because we'll be playing till tomorrow morning, since our Santa comes tonight," said Phil.

In his excitement, Bear pushed his furry muzzle too far into the railing, so he almost fell through.

"Did you hear that Nosey. Just like us, they're celebrating Christmas tonight, too. This is even better than I'd hoped for."

In a few moments, Bear was sailing on his special dreamboat, imagining them all celebrating Christmas together, when Nosey interrupted his dreams and poked him to pay attention to the conversation downstairs.

"If we went over for an hour or two, we would still have enough time after four to decorate the tree and to prepare..." said Phil.

"Then let's grab their gift and go over," they heard Hanna's cheerful voice and soon they heard the familiar click of the lock.

"Nosey, we have at least an hour. Let's go down and check out what these guys are up to."

Nosey didn't need any further encouragement; he was on his way down, flapping up a storm with his ears.

Part 2

The animals saw the most majestic Christmas tree towering in the middle of the living room. The air was filled with the fragrance of moist, fresh-cut fir, the kind you can only smell at Christmas time.

"WOW!!!" the animals said. They saw boxes and boxes of Christmas tree decorations, all around the tree, waiting to be placed in their own special spot.

"Nosey, I have a great idea." and Nosey loved it when his friend started out like this, because it was always followed by tons of fun.

"We could decorate the Christmas tree for them, and then we would become a part of their Christmas miracle, because they'd never find out it was us who did it."

Nosey improvised a weird elephant dance. He was very happy and excited.

"OK, Nosey, what do you think of this?"

"In order to decorate this beautiful tree, we'll have to come up with ingenious ways to reach the branches. You see, if we climb up, we may topple the tree over. We are mighty giants of the jungle after all, and this is no time to get into trouble," said Bear, in all seriousness.

We can reach the lower branches by jumping, but then we

have the problem of the higher branches and the treetop. Luckily, the Christmas lights are already on. Let's run around a bit and look for stuff that can help us decorate. See you back here in ten minutes, OK?" With these words Bear McQueen was gone in a flash and out of sight.

The animals ran around for a few minutes and collected things they thought would come in handy, such as a fishing rod, a LEGO construction set, a bow and some foam arrows, a rocket launching pad and two badminton rackets.

"OK, Nosey, let's start," said Bear with excitement. They worked with such speed that Santa's elves couldn't have done a better job, themselves.

Bear was reeling hangers up with the fishing rod for Nosey, who was seated on top of a LEGO structure, right next to the tree. He hung the decorations carefully with his trunk. Later, they used the bow and arrow to land some silver stars on the hard to reach branches, and even launched a few gold cones with the badminton rackets. Finally, they used the rocket launching pad to place the Christmas tree topper on the tree.

Just then, they heard "cuckoo, cuckoo, cuckoo, cuckoo." Luckily, they were done decorating.

"Wow, Nosey, we've done a great job!" said Bear, as they collapsed in a giddy pile, looking up at the beautifully decorated tree. They sat there for a while, but knew they'd soon have to return to their hiding spot, so they did.

They sat in the treasure chest room in silence for what seemed like hours, until Bear could take it no longer

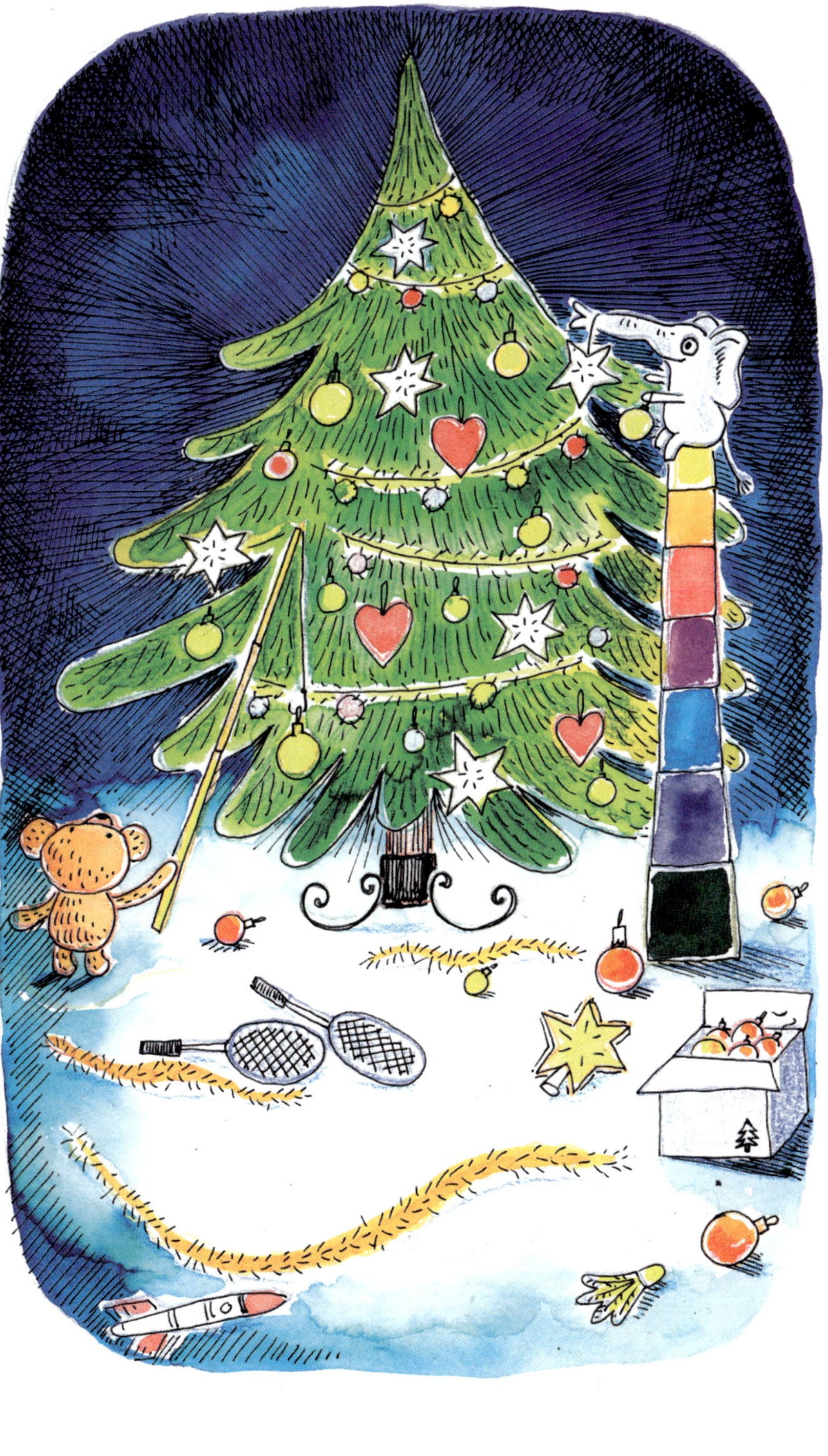

and said, "OK, Nosey, let's celebrate Christmas. This time we won't be under a Christmas tree, but at least, we're surrounded by lots of toys. If we perch up on the windowsill, we can choose a beautiful, illuminated fir from the backyard. We'll call that our Christmas tree. "Let's display our presents and then we'll play, OK? C'mon, Nosey, don't be sad. It is Christmas Eve, after all!"

Nosey half-heartedly flapped his right ear, in agreement.

"OK. Remember, we have to decide who places his presents last. Can I be the last one this time?" he asked, really hoping that it would be OK with his friend.

Nosey nodded happily, because this year he could wrap everything up, unlike last Christmas, when he made a beautiful spinning carousel for his friend that had to be displayed. The rule was that the person who had something to display put out his presents last. This way, no surprise was ever ruined.

"Great. I really need to be the last one." Bear said, thinking of the hot air balloon that just had to be hung. There was no other way.

Nosey pushed a tiny bell ornament he had found to the window and both animals were extremely happy, because the ringing of the bell was a very important part of their Christmas traditions. It always signaled the start of their celebrations.

Bear went into the chest and closed his eyes while Nosey got the presents and arranged them on the windowsill. He then jumped into the treasure chest and poked his

friend to let him know it was his turn. Bear did a great job with the hot air balloon display and carefully laid out his other presents, under the balloon. After he was done, he lit a small candle and rang the tiny bell. Nosey jumped out of the treasure chest, carrying a sparkling musical Christmas card. He perched up beside Bear and opened it, and Jingle Bells started playing. But he no longer paid attention to the music, because he noticed the hot air balloon hanging from the window frame. He was absolutely fascinated by hot air balloons, and he was so awed by its beauty that he didn't even flap his ears. He edged closer, as if in a trance, to check it out. The cold winter breeze moved it just a tiny bit, as it was hanging. Nosey hugged his friend, who encouraged him to get still closer. He wanted Nosey to discover the special surprise, inside.

Sure enough, Nosey found a magical blue marble in the gondola, just like his favourite one in the toy store he always guarded with such care. He lost it on their way over the ocean and had been quietly sad about it ever since. Of course, what he didn't know was that Bear had found it in the airplane and decided to surprise him with it.

"C'mon, Nosey. It's your marble. I found it for you!"

"Thanks, Bear," he whispered gratefully and hugged his friend, tightly. He was eager to see how Bear would like the presents he had prepared for him, so he nudged Bear to open the first gift.

"Wow, Nosey! This is fantastic! I'd almost forgotten how much we used to play Nine Men's Morris. This is wonderful. We can play till dawn."

Taking turns, the animals soon opened everything: the Mikado Sticks, the snowflake card, the sleigh and the airplane.

They were swimming in joy. Nosey opened the card occasionally, flapped his big ears around and went back to play with his friend. Bear was a little better at playing Nine Men's Morris than Nosey, but then Nosey was very careful and patient, so he could usually pick up more Mikado sticks than Bear, without disturbing the pile.

Just when Nosey bent forward to pick up another stick, they heard steps running up the stairs. This interrupted their celebration, and all they had time for was to dive off the windowsill.

"Oh, my," whispered Bear, hanging on to Nosey. "What did we jump in-to-to-to?" Bear asked, trying hard to finish his sentence, as he felt that they were being lifted up and flown down the two flights of stairs.

"Nosey," whispered Bear almost inaudibly. "We're downstairs. I can smell the fir."

From that moment on, things started happening so fast that Bear McQueen and Nosey could hardly follow the pace of action happening around them.

For all the years to come, they would tell each other what had happened that very special night, so they could relive the moments, over and over again, in slow motion.

"We almost forgot to bring down the gift bag that Melanie's mom gave us," they heard, as Hanna removed the red tissue from the gift bag and peeked into it curiously.

"Look, Phil!" she exclaimed as she pulled out Bear, who was upside down, dragging a very startled Nosey by his left paw.

Bear looked at his new master, with eyes wider than ever, his extremities, motionless, like a star. The world was upside down, but it felt just the way it should be. As she turned him around, Bear let out a squeaky, high-pitched

"Here I am, Bear
and this is my friend Nosey.
Merry Christmas!"

What really happened that night will remain a mystery, forever.

Hanna remembers hugging both animals, and saying "Hi, guys," and saying something like "Phil, we got a bear and an elephant from Melanie's mom. Aren't they adorable?" not quite understanding how and why these two rag animals touched her heart instantly, but recalling her dear bear from her childhood, and somehow feeling cozy and just right. She remembers Bear McQueen's twinkling greenish brown eyes that were not so mischievous now, rather just very touched and a little hazy, extremely happy and full of expectation.

Phil remembers looking at his wife and seeing how happy she was, deciding not to tell her how unpredictable bears were and the amount of trouble they could cause no matter how you try to tame them. Nosey remembers how they all crept under the Christmas tree, where they started up the electric train set. Then they played with the mini ping-pong set, and later they opened the kaleidoscope making kit. Since they didn't want to start up any major projects that night, they decided that they would build the roman clock the following day, along with the two model rockets. Nosey also remembers finding a light-up ball under the tree that no one seemed to claim and so it became his. He still keeps it carefully tucked away, with his blue marble, in a special box.

Bear remembers whispering, "Nosey, this is incredible. I think she likes us. Phil is looking at us a bit suspiciously, but he may just be jealous." And he remembers Nosey nodding and agreeing that that was very likely.

Both animals clearly remember swimming in true Christmas spirit and wishing those moments would never end. They remember the Christmas tree hangers spinning above their heads, sparkling in the flames of the fireplace, mixed with the colourful Christmas lights. They remember how their thoughts and feelings were spinning until they felt dizzy.

Bear remembers clearly how they played for hours and hours, and when it was almost dawn, Phil suggested that they roast chestnuts on the barbeque outside, and since enough snow had fallen in the meantime, he pulled everyone around in a blue sled. At the end, they all collapsed, deliriously happy around the Christmas tree.

That night Bear looked up at the Little Dipper, and whispered almost inaudibly, "Thank you, Santa!"

He was very touched and held on tight to Nosey because he knew that from now on, they would be part of a family, a loving, caring family, where they would always be the star attraction. They could produce all the mischievous tricks a bear and elephant could ever dream up, and they would have a chance to argue with their masters, tease them relentlessly, and never stop laughing and jumping and laughing and just having the most unimaginable fun time a bear and an elephant could have in a family.

Forever.

CONTENTS

Chapter One
Bear McQueen and Nosey Land in Burlington

Part 1 5
Part 2 13

Chapter Two
Bear Detective Investigates

Part 1 18
Part 2 25

Chapter Three
Nosey is Lost!

Part 1 35
Part 2 45

Chapter Four
Skating under the Stars

Part 1 56
Part 2 62

Chapter Five
Midnight Adventure

Part 1 _____ 71
Part 2 _____ 79
Part 3 _____ 82

Chapter Six
Trip to Niagara Falls

Part 1 _____ 88
Part 2 _____ 95
Part 3 _____ 104

Chapter Seven
Here I am Bear!

Part 1 _____ 112
Part 2 _____ 119

Acknowledgements

I would like to thank my family first and foremost
for always supporting me and keeping the spirit of this book
alive throughout my childhood into my adult years.
I must say a massive thank you to
the following incredible people:
Natalia Tukhareli, who believed that this book should be
published after reading the first drafts years ago.
Kay Brenders, for her insightful edits
and for cheering me along the way.
Niki Stamatelos, for guiding me with style choices
and for her relentless support.
Julia Keech, for her enthusiasm and her belief
in the success of this book.
Jacqueline Molnár, for bringing Bear and Nosey to life
through her fantastic illustrations and without whom this book
could not have been published.
David Torrents, for all the precision and design.
Bizou Philipp, for her incredible insights and edits
and her magical personality and love.
Huge thank you, to all my friends,
and thanks to Bear and Nosey!

Copyright © 2020 by Gwim Philipp
Illustrations copyright © 2020 by Jacqueline Molnár
All rights reserved.

Published by Gwim Philipp
No part of this book may be used or reproduced
in any manner whatsoever without the prior
written permission of the authors, except
in the case of brief quotations embodied in reviews.

www.gwimphilipp.com
www.jacquelinemolnar.com

Manufactured by Amazon.ca
Bolton, ON